A Race with the Devil

Allison skidded wildly as her Halloween bag jerked tight across her chest. She and the bike crashed to the street, and the bag's contents flew into the air. Allison gasped in pain.

Joe and Frank sprinted after the mugger.

"Hey you!" Joe called. "Stop!"

The bandit stopped, but only long enough to scoop up a few of the spilled envelopes. The black-robed devil then turned and ran into the alley across the street.

"Look after Allison," Frank called to Callie. "We'll catch the thief."

Callie Shaw ran to where Allison had fallen. "I'm all right," the girl in the witch costume said, "just a bit shaken up." She and Callie lifted the bike and began to pick up the spilled clues.

Frank and Joe charged into the alley after the bandit. "Any idea who we're chasing?" Joe asked.

"Between the darkness and the mask, who knows?" Frank replied.

The Hardy Boys Mystery Stories

Available from ALADDIN Paperbacks

THE HARDY BOYS®

#175
TRICK-OR-TROUBLE

FRANKLIN W. DIXON

Aladdin Paperbacks
New York London Toronto Sydney Singapore

First Aladdin Paperbacks edition September 2002

Copyright © 2002 by Simon & Schuster, Inc.

ALADDIN PAPERBACKS
An imprint of Simon & Schuster
Children's Publishing Division
1230 Avenue of the Americas
New York, NY 10020

The text of this book was set in New Caledonia.

Printed in the United States of America
2   4   6   8   10   9   7   5   3   1

THE HARDY BOYS MYSTERY STORIES is a trademark
of Simon & Schuster, Inc.

THE HARDY BOYS and colophon are registered trademarks
of Simon & Schuster, Inc.

Library of Congress Control Number 2002103779

ISBN: 0-7434-3759-4

Contents

1 Fright Night

"My mom is driving me nuts!" Daphne Soesbee complained. She and her four friends walked down Racine Street—away from Java John's and back toward the Book Bank—their arms brimming with carry-out food and drinks.

"I thought going a little crazy was a *good* thing during Halloween," Joe Hardy said. He hefted the large bag of sandwiches in his broad arms and smiled.

Daphne crinkled her nose at him and turned to the dark-haired girl walking beside her. "Iola, tell your boyfriend that he has a weird sense of humor."

Iola Morton laughed. "He's the *detective*," she said, "I think he can figure it out for himself."

Daphne laughed too. She struggled with the tray

1

of drinks she was carrying, trying not to spill.

"I can take that," Chet Morton offered, reaching for the tray. He already held two bags of carry-out food in his big hands.

Daphne smiled at him. "I don't see how," she said, "unless you have some hidden talent for juggling."

"Chet has many talents," Frank Hardy said, "most of them hidden."

Chet, a big guy, grinned back at the older Hardy. "I'll tackle both you and your smart aleck brother after we drop this grub off at the Book Bank."

"Oh, no," Callie Shaw said. She shook her blond head and wagged her finger at him. "You're not about to fight with my boyfriend when you *promised* to help your sister and Daphne and Daphne's mom with this contest. Work first; fight later."

"I can do both," Chet said. "I'm a man of many talents."

"Most of them hidden," Iola Morton added, giggling.

"So, is it the Halloween contest that's making your mom crazy, Daphne?" Frank asked.

Daphne nodded. "She's almost wishing she'd never agreed to write the clues when the Bayport Merchants Association asked her. It's a lot of work."

"Which is why my sister, Callie, and I are here to help," Chet said gallantly.

"Mom and I appreciate your volunteering," Daphne

2

said. "If you can handle some of the gofer work, that'll give us time to concentrate on the contest."

"Did the clue cards come in yet?" Chet asked.

"We got them last night," Daphne replied. "Mom and I ran the first day's envelopes out to the participating merchants this morning. I had to take the day off from school, but . . ." She shrugged. "What's a girl to do?"

"What about the clues for the other four days?" Joe asked.

Iola tousled her boyfriend's blond hair. "Trying to gain some advantage in the contest, Joe Hardy?" she asked.

"Just curious about the mechanics of it all," Joe said.

"My mom can fill you in while we eat," Daphne said. "You deserve a sandwich or two, since you helped lug this 'feast' here."

They hauled the food to the front entrance of the Book Bank. The store was a tall, narrow building with big plate-glass windows on either side of the door. Books and decorations for the "Halloween Spooktacular," as the contest was called, lined the display windows. Cobwebs hung from the rafters, and a giant papier-mâché spider crawled among the volumes near the front of the glass. The word "Book" in the big sign above the door had been painted over in dripping red letters with the word "Blood."

"Nice touch," Frank noted.

"Mom thought it gave the store the proper atmosphere for the *Spooktacular*," Daphne replied.

Chet opened the door, and all six teens went inside. A bell rang as they entered.

Long ago the store had been an actual, working bank. Its solid brick construction harkened back to the beginning of the twentieth century. The building had remained a bank until the end of the nineteen sixties, when they built a new branch near the Bayport courthouse. The building's former owners had added plate-glass windows when they turned it into a retail establishment.

Daphne's mom, Kathryn Soesbee, had remodeled it again when she bought the place a little over two years ago. Bookshelves lined the interior of the building. The first floor was taken up with new stock, while the second was devoted to old books and rare editions. A metal spiral staircase near the center of the store led up to the second floor.

Despite the renovations, the original bank vault still existed. It was a big, thick-walled room near the back of the first floor. The vault looked like something out of a TV western series. It had a tiny, barred window in one wall near the ceiling. The Soesbees used it mostly for storage.

As the friends entered the store and set down their carry-out bags on a glass-topped table near the checkout counter, Kathryn Soesbee bustled out of the vault. She was taller and slimmer than Daphne, though both mother and daughter shared the same dark red hair. She looked harried, and almost surprised to see everyone.

"Back already?" she said. "Great, 'cause I've got a million things for us to do."

"I thought the contest wasn't starting until midnight," Joe said, checking his watch. "It's barely seven now."

"There's so much final preparation work to do!" Ms. Soesbee said. "I have to coordinate with the merchant's committee, call the media, fix up the store displays and . . ."

"Eat first," Daphne said. "Nervous breakdown later."

"It's easier to really go crazy on a full stomach," Chet said, smiling.

Ms. Soesbee let out a long sigh. "You're right. I've been working too hard. I just want everything to be *perfect* for this contest."

"I doubt anyone expects perfection," Frank said, "just fun."

"With the haunted house for a kickoff event and the Halloween parade at the end," Callie added, "it's sure to be the best contest Bayport has ever seen." She and the others sat down at the table, and Daphne doled out food.

Kathryn Soesbee sat down as well, though she drummed her fingers nervously on the tabletop.

"My mother," Daphne said, rolling her eyes, "the madwoman of Marketing Street."

Ms. Soesbee looked over at her daughter. "So," she said, looking at Frank, Joe, and Callie, "are you three looking forward to the contest?"

"Very much," Frank nodded.

"We're excited to see what kind of puzzles you've cooked up," Callie added.

"I hope they'll be good enough," Ms. Soesbee said. "The Merchants Association has a lot riding on this."

"Chill, Mom," Daphne said. "The riddles are great. They'll keep this town jumping right up to Halloween."

"With your literary knowledge and your daughter's gaming skills, it's a sure bet," Chet said, smiling at Daphne.

Ms. Soesbee sighed. "I wish I were so confident," she said, "but it's all so complicated, coordinating the committee, the media, the participating merchants, the stores providing the prizes, the zoo supplying creepy animals. . . ."

"There are prizes?" Chet said, surprised. "Maybe I shouldn't have volunteered to help out. Then I'd still be able to win something."

Iola rapped lightly on her brother's head with one knuckle. "You have to solve the puzzles first, bro."

"Hey, I've hung around with Joe and Frank

6

enough," Chet said, mocking defensiveness. "I've won my share of puzzle-based games."

"Not against me," Daphne said with a smile.

"There are instant prizes, too," Ms. Soesbee said. "Anyone can win just by visiting one of the participating merchants and picking up a clue envelope. Of course, you *do* have to solve puzzles to get the *best* prizes."

"What are the chances that one of the big prizes will turn up right away?" Frank asked.

"No chance at all," Daphne said. "The clues that lead to the big stuff are stretched out over the whole contest. People will have to really scramble to scoop them all up by the last day."

"And I'm sure you've made them really hard to figure out," Joe said.

Daphne smiled. "I guess you'll find out, won't you."

"What happens to the prizes no one wins?" Callie asked.

"Well, the contest guarantees that the grand prize—the reconditioned RV mobile home—will be awarded," Ms. Soesbee said, "but the rest go back to their sponsoring merchants. A lot of merchants are holding a second-chance raffle for unclaimed prizes.

"I'm not handling that part of the contest; it's been left to the individual stores. I've got enough to worry about! Speaking of which, we should get back to work. Which bag has the cookies in it? I'll set them behind the counter for tonight."

Chet handed her one of the bags he'd been carrying.

"Better check those," Joe said with a smile. "Some might have wandered off."

"Wander off *yourself*, Hardy," Chet replied. "Unless you want to pitch in, and not participate in the contest."

"No chance of that," Callie said. "Joe and Frank promised we could enter this as a team."

"We're still figuring out a way to split that mobile home, though," Frank said.

"You're not the only brain in town, Frank Hardy," Daphne replied good-naturedly. "It's just possible that someone *else* may win the grand prize."

Frank smiled. "Possible," he said.

"But not likely," Joe added.

Callie hooked her arms through the brothers' elbows. "If you need your boyfriend, Iola," she said, "he'll be home plotting strategies for tonight's big kickoff."

Joe, Frank, and Callie picked up the Hardys' van from the alley behind the building and headed home. They stopped at Callie's house so she could pick up her costume for the opening shindig at the old Niles mansion. Joe wasn't dressing up, but Callie had convinced Frank to go as a gypsy rogue; she would be wearing a fortune-teller costume.

The kickoff party started at ten P.M., with the official contest beginning at midnight and running until one A.M. The following four days, the contest would start at dusk and run until midnight.

"This seems like a pretty risky venture," Callie said, adjusting the fall of her long gypsy skirt. "Since you don't have to buy anything to participate, the merchants could lose a lot of money."

"Most of the prizes aren't big enough to affect a store's bottom line," Joe said.

"You can only get one free entry per store per night," Frank said. "But I read in the paper that you can get bonus entries for purchases. That should stimulate sales." He smeared some dark makeup on his chin to simulate beard stubble.

Callie nodded. "I guess pulling people into the stores may lead to actual shopping." She put her arm around Frank's shoulder and posed. "What do you think, Joe?"

"A perfect gypsy couple," Joe replied.

"You sure you won't join us?" Frank asked. "Every good gypsy couple needs a werewolf for a pet."

Joe shook his head. "Iola doesn't go for beards."

They said good night to Mr. and Mrs. Hardy, and headed up to the old Niles place.

The Niles mansion sat on the corner of Weis Parkway and Hickman Drive, near the southern edge of downtown. It was perched on a small hill behind a stone wall that was topped with metal

9

spikes. The big iron gate at the front entrance stood ajar, and overgrown bushes crowded the driveway. Someone had put up a sawhorse barricade just inside the gate, so people wouldn't bring their cars up to the house.

The Hardys and Callie found a parking spot a block away, and they hiked back to the mansion.

"It's like something out of a horror movie," Callie said as they walked through the gate and around the barricade.

The mansion's Victorian towers stretched like broken fingers toward the cloudy sky. Its clapboards were gray and weather-beaten; some of its shutters hung loose alongside their windows. Though the long walk to the huge front doors was lit by jack-o'-lanterns, no light came from within the manor.

"I read the historical society is renovating the place in conjunction with the contest," Frank said.

"If that's true," Joe said, "they haven't gotten very far."

"Or they're really bad at renovation," Callie added with a nervous grin.

They walked up to the big oak doors, and Frank lifted the gargoyle-faced iron knocker. He thumped the knocker down three times. The sound echoed eerily through the ancient house.

"Just like a Karloff flick," Joe said.

Frank cocked his head and listened. "Is that wolves I hear howling?"

As he spoke, one of the heavy oaken doors creaked open and a pale, wizened face peered out.

Callie's eyes went wide and she gasped. "But . . . you're dead!"

2 The Old Dark House

The flickering candelabra in the old man's hand cast weird light across his strange, menacing face. The man's thin lips pulled back in a smile, revealing pointed teeth. Terrified screams from inside the mansion drifted out through the doorway. Beyond the leering figure were many dark shadows in a cavernous room.

Callie put her hand to her mouth, stifling a scream. The face in the door laughed.

"Chill, Callie," Joe said. "It's just Vincent Blasko—the old horror movie star."

"B-but, he's dead," Callie said. "I read about it in the papers."

"You shouldn't believe everything you read, young lady," Blasko replied. "Like Mark Twain, reports of my death have been greatly exaggerated. The newspapers printed a retraction, but . . ." He shrugged. "No one ever reads the back pages."

Frank put his hand on his girlfriend's shoulder. "You must have missed the publicity about Mr. Blasko hosting this event," he said.

Callie nodded nervously. "I was so busy working on the parade float, I must have," she replied. She forced a smile. "You really gave me quite a scare."

Mr. Blasko grinned back. "I have that effect upon people. One of the consequences of playing so many mad doctors and vampires, I suppose."

"Well," Callie said, "I am *really* glad you're not dead."

"As am I," Blasko replied. "Playing a ghoul all these years probably made it easier for people to believe that I had passed on. Plus, I haven't appeared in many films in recent years—not enough good scripts, you know. My career was in decline before my 'death' and since . . . Well, let's just say that no one's beating down the cemetery gates to hire me."

"You're the perfect host for this, though," Frank said.

"Ah!" Blasko said, "I've dropped out of character!" He held up his small candelabra and raised his cloak over the lower half of his face. "Welcome to the *Halloween Spooktacular.* I am your ghostly host, Vincent Blasko. Won't you please . . . step inside?" He backed away from the door, opening it just wide enough so that the teens could squeeze through.

The door opened into a wide foyer lit by flickering, electric candles. Long streamers of fake cobwebs hung from the ceiling. The bats on the far side of the room were real; they were actually in a long cage near the top of the wall. The shadows in the room though, concealed the cage's frame, as well as the wire holding the bats inside. A stern-looking lady ghoul stood guard to one side of the cage.

"On loan from the zoo, I bet," Frank said.

Joe and Callie nodded.

Several large black loudspeakers produced the screams the three friends had heard from outside. The noise effectively concealed the din from the party in the next room.

Stepping past Mr. Blasko, the three teens entered the main hall of the Niles mansion. The room was huge, but people filled almost every inch of the floor. The large stairways on either side of the room had been roped off, and a large "security ghoul" stood watch beside each one.

Leering plastic jack-o'-lanterns along the baseboards provided much of the room's light. The rest came from ornamental brass light stands and candelabras fitted with flickering electric candle bulbs. All the windows of the room had been covered with heavy fire curtains.

"That explains why we didn't see any lights from outside," Joe said.

On the far side of the chamber, an old grand-father clock stood against the wall, and a sign reading HALLOWEEN SPOOKTACULAR BLASTOFF BASH hung from the ceiling. A DJ platform had been set up below the sign, between two huge speaker stacks. A woman in a werewolf mask stood near the microphone, enthusiastically spinning discs. An eerie mix of techno pop, creepy classical music, horror movie soundtracks, and Halloween novelty tunes filled the room. Anxious contestants, some in costume, danced to the throbbing, pulselike beat.

Most of the dancers seemed to be in their teens or twenties, though there were also clusters of older people and younger kids. The three friends recognized some of their classmates and acquaintances among the group.

As the Hardys and Callie drank in the whole scene, a witch with long strawberry-blond hair brushed past. "I suspected I'd find you here," the witch said, eyeing the Hardys suspiciously.

Joe laughed. "Good to see you, too, Allison. Frank, Callie, this is Allison Rosenberg—she's in Mr. Pane's lit class with me. Allison, my older brother, Frank, and Callie Shaw."

"I recognized Allison," Frank said, extending his hand to her. "You really scored for Bayport High at that last math meet."

Allison shook Frank's hand and gave a curt nod. "I'm surprised a sports hero like you would notice," she said with a wry smile.

Callie put her hand on Frank's shoulder. "There's more to Frank Hardy than the best throwing arm in Bayport."

"I'm sure there is," Allison replied. "Have you signed in yet?"

Frank, Joe, and Callie shook their heads.

Allison pointed to a table set up near one of the stairways. Two lady vampires in bloodstained wedding dresses manned the table, handing out papers and taking applications. "Better get to it before the last-minute rush," she said. "Good luck with the contest." She moved through the crowd and onto the dance floor.

"She's the smartest girl in school," Callie said as they edged their way toward the sign-up table. "She could give us some real competition."

"I expect there'll be plenty of competition all around," Joe said. "It's not just teenagers trying to win. We're competing with some of the most clever people in the city."

"And some troublemakers as well," Frank added. "Look." He angled his head toward a couple of kids dressed in leather who were hanging out in a corner of the room.

"Missy Gates and Jay Stone," Callie said. "Do you think the rest of the 'Kings' are in on this, too?"

"Could be," Joe replied. The Kings were a self-styled cybergang who also dabbled in cars and motorcycles. They'd given the Hardys some trouble before. Gates and Stone didn't notice the Hardys in the crowd.

"Let's hope they keep to themselves this time," Frank added.

The three teens arrived at the registration table and got their sign-up forms from one of Dracula's brides. They filled out the information, and then gave the papers back to the vampire, who gave them official contestant badges and a rules folder. The woman behind the table smiled, showing her fangs, and said, "Have a superspooky night!"

As they walked away from the table, a big guy wearing a football uniform bumped into Joe. The kid was tall and muscular with curly black hair and an angular face. "Watch where you're going, Hardy," the boy said.

"Watch it yourself, Brent," Joe replied. Brent Jackson and Joe played opposite each other on the Bayport High football team. "Very original costume," Joe added, clearly meaning just the opposite.

"When you've got it, flaunt it," Jackson said. "Nice costume yourself. The 'down 'n' out' look suits you. I see you've brought your brother and his girl for escorts. Did Iola finally dump you, or is this party too late for her?"

"Actually," Joe said, keeping his temper in check, "I'm working."

"Oh yeah?" Jackson replied.

"I'm helping the zookeepers round up stray animals," Joe said. "Since you're a 'friend,' I'll look the other way so you can lope back into your cage before anyone spots you."

Callie laughed.

"Very funny," Jackson sneered.

"What are you up to, Brent, besides looking for trouble?" Frank added.

"Trouble I don't need," Jackson countered. "It's *prizes* I'm into. But I just can't resist needling you Hardy boys. I bet I score more swag in this contest than you hotshots do."

"Ha!" Callie said.

"Lucky for you we're not betting men," Joe said.

"Lucky for your wallets, you mean," Jackson replied.

"We'll see how it turns out when the contest is over," Frank said.

Jackson smiled and nodded. "You bet we will." He turned and slipped into the crowd.

"Don't trip over any big words," Callie called after him.

"Halloween must bring the creeps out of the woodwork," Joe said.

"Come on," Frank replied, "let's grab a snack before the big blastoff."

"How about a dance first?" Callie asked, taking Frank by the elbow.

"You two hit the dance floor," Joe said. "I'll round up some food."

"Good plan," Frank replied. He took Callie's arm and the two of them joined the costumed crowd.

Joe dodged his way through the other contestants to the refreshment table on the side of the room. A thin black-haired teen in jeans and a denim jacket turned and nodded at him as he approached.

"What's up, Joe?"

"Just waiting for the action to start, Ren," Joe replied.

Ren Takei took a sip of his soda. "Me, too," he said.

"I see you're not in costume either," Joe said.

"A costume would just slow me down."

"What kind of prizes are you looking to score?"

"The usual," Ren replied. "Electronics, music— anything expensive." He shrugged. "I'm not too picky."

Joe laughed. "I doubt that," he said. Ren was known around school for his top-of-the-line gadgets.

"Hey, any prize can be cashed in or traded up," Ren replied. "You and Frank both in on this?"

Joe nodded.

"I'll keep out of your way then," Ren said. "I know how competitive you guys are."

"Frank and me?" Joe asked, feigning innocence.

Ren laughed. "I'll catch you later."

"See you." Joe turned away and ordered some soda and pizza slices from the food stand.

By the time he fought his way back to the edge of the dance floor, Frank and Callie were ready for a break. They found a quiet spot near a wall and ate.

As they were finishing their food, Vincent Blasko stepped to the podium. The werewolf DJ cranked down the music.

"Good eeeeevening!" Blasko said in a fake Hungarian accent.

"Good eeeeevening!" the crowd hollered back.

"Welcome to the Bayport Merchants Association's First Annual Halloween Spoooooktacular!" Blasko said. He waited for the applause to die down and then continued. "Before we start this macabre contest, there's something I'd like to say . . ." He looked around as though about to confide a great secret, then leaned close to the mike and shouted, "BOO!"

Most of the room jumped. Then everyone burst into laughter and applauded again.

"As you probably know, I am Vincent Blasko, and I will be your horrifying host for the duration of this fright fest."

Everyone applauded politely.

"Cut to the chase!" Ren Takei called from the back of the room.

Blasko grinned, showing his fangs. "Ah . . .

'Chase' and 'cut' . . . two words very dear to my heart. Perhaps the young man would like to stop by my graveyard later so that I may demonstrate."

The audience hooted and laughed and Ren crept away into the shadows.

"Before the bloodletting begins, though," Blasko continued, "I have a few announcements. First, any of you who have not yet registered to compete in the contest may want to do so now. It is free and won't take too much of your time—providing you stay out of biting distance of my 'brides.' If not . . ." He shrugged. "Well, it may cost you a pint or two. And I'm not talking about milk!

"Second, if you do not register tonight, you may register at any of the participating merchants in downtown Bayport at any time during the contest, or at the Chamber of Commerce during regular business hours. You need to register to be eligible to collect clues and win Spooktacular prizes."

"What kind of prizes?" Missy Gates called out from near the exit.

"I'm so glad you asked," Blasko said, pulling a sheet of paper out of his cloak and studying it. "Among the amazing items to be won are . . . CDs, MP3 players, a stereo system, pagers, clothing, a leather jacket, dinners out, a cell phone, a classic VW Beetle . . ."

"A junk car, you mean!" Jay Stone, standing next to Missy, shouted out.

The crowd laughed, but Blasko continued. "A computer system; a new, limited edition Geronimo motorcycle; a sailboat; and the grand prize, a reconditioned Waukesha mobile home RV! As well as many other astounding prizes.

"Third, each participating merchant will have five different clues each day of the Spooktacular—but the clues will *only* be given out during special Spooktacular hours: from midnight to one A.M. tonight, and from dusk to midnight for the rest of the week." The movie star grinned again. "We wouldn't want any of our contestants caught out in the sunlight, would we?"

"He's really into this," Callie whispered to Joe and Frank.

"What do you expect?" Joe replied. "Blasko's been doing this kind of thing since before any of us were born."

"Before our parents were born, too," Frank added.

"Each registered contestant can receive one free clue, per day, from each participating store," Blasko continued. "The other clues may be obtained by making special purchases within the store.

"To win the prizes, you *must* present all the pertinent clues to the store awarding the prize. Clues for the major prizes must be presented to the Judging Committee. See your packets for more details about this.

"Some clues will be found during the treasure

hunt phase, and will not be given out by stores. Even if you stumble across a big prize, you may *not* claim it without showing the proper—and legal—chain of clues! Anyone attempting to do so will be thrown to the werewolves."

The werewolf DJ standing nearby threw back her head and howled into her mike.

Blasko laughed along with the audience. "And on that note," he said, "it's time to check the official Spooktacular countdown." He gazed at the moldering grandfather clock behind him and smiled.

"My timing is excellent, as ever. It's only moments before the witching hour! If you will all count down the last minute with me. . . . Sixty . . . fifty-nine . . ."

The crowd joined in. "Fifty-eight, fifty-seven, fifty-six . . ."

"What store do you want to go to first?" Callie asked.

"I think the Soesbees would be insulted if we didn't start with the Book Bank," Frank said.

Callie smiled. "That makes sense."

"Thirteen . . . twelve . . . eleven . . ."

When the crowd reached eleven, the lights suddenly went out.

As the room plunged into darkness, someone screamed. "The bats! They're loose!"

3 Severed Head Start

Leathery wings fluttered softly, and more screams filled the room. People began to push and shove each other in the darkness. A thin ray of light flashed as the front door opened in the hallway beyond. Someone had slipped out.

"Don't panic!" Frank called out. "The bats see better in here than we do!"

"He's right!" called a woman's voice. The Hardys and Callie assumed it was one of the zookeepers who were tending the bats. "The bats won't hit you if you stand still. They're harmless. Milling around could hurt *them* or cause them to hit something!"

Her words calmed the crowd a bit, but several scared partyers slipped out the exit. In the darkened room, people pulled out cigarette lighters and matches and lit them. Frank and Joe pulled out tiny flashlights from their pockets.

"Where'd you get those?" Callie asked. She stood close to Frank and glanced apprehensively at the flying bats.

"We brought them for the treasure hunt," Joe replied.

In the dim light, Vincent Blasko raised his hands and spoke in a loud, theatrical voice. He ignored the bats darting overhead and the two zookeepers chasing them with fine mesh nets.

"Remain calm!" Blasko said. "The bats are our friends—well, *my* friends, anyway. What spookier way to start the Spooktacular? Please remain calm while our security people restore power and recapture our winged allies."

The DJ appeared with Blasko's small candelabra. "Now," Blasko said, "isn't that better? I don't know about you, but I feel quite at home." He chuckled menacingly; the audience laughed nervously in response. "This reminds me of my trip to Dracula's castle, in the Romanian province formerly known as Transylvania. . . ."

Before he could finish the anecdote, though, the lights came back on. Blasko smiled. "Ah! There we are. Why do you all look so pale? Have my 'brides' been stealing a few donations?"

With the lights back on, the audience laughed more boldly. One of the zookeepers sidled up to

Blasko and whispered in his ear. Blasko nodded and then spoke again. "Our friends from the zoo have asked that we take extra precautions as we leave the building, so that none of their leather-winged charges can make good on this attempted jailbreak." He smiled, showing his pointed teeth.

"So, with the witching hour passed, and if you will proceed to the exits with caution, I now declare the Halloween Spooktacular contest open! Be sure to visit my film festival at the Browning Theater and pick up your free clue! Happy hunting!" With a flourish of his cape, Blasko turned away from the microphone and spoke to a member of the Chamber of Commerce contest committee.

"Oh," Blasko said, returning to the mike, "in all the excitement I almost forgot." He held up a ceramic jack-o'-lantern a bit larger than a softball. "These finely crafted pumpkins can be found at the sites of many major clues. Treat their contents carefully, as they may lead you to other clues or instant prizes. Remember, you need a legal chain of clues to collect your prizes. Play fairly! You never know when the cadaver cops may be watching!"

Callie, the Hardys, and the rest of the crowd in the main hall filed toward the door in a more or less orderly manner.

"Some spooky accident," Callie said.

"I doubt it was an accident," Frank replied.

Callie looked puzzled. "Why would someone

turn out the lights and let the bats loose?"

Joe checked his watch. "It's ten past midnight now—and it'll take at least another five minutes to get out the door without letting the bats escape."

"Someone got a nice head start," Frank added.

"I don't see Missy Gates or Jay Stone around," Joe said.

"They could have left during the commotion," Frank replied. "The door opened a couple of times while it was dark. I'm betting whoever threw the circuit breaker and let the bats loose was the first one out."

"It would have been easy for Missy and Jay to pull it off working together," Callie suggested.

"Remember, there were a lot of people here that we don't know anything about, either," Joe said.

"But we know that Missy, Jay, and their friends are troublemakers," Callie said.

"They were here, that's for sure," Frank replied.

By the time they exited the old mansion, downtown Bayport was already crawling with prize hunters. Many of the contestants who were bustling through the streets were dressed in their Halloween outfits; anyone wearing a costume got a discount at certain shops.

Callie spotted Allison Rosenberg in her witch costume, flitting from one shop to the next, picking up free clues. Her Halloween bag already looked stuffed with clue envelopes.

"Looks like Allison's had a good start," Callie said.

"Maybe too good," Joe noted.

"You think she might have caused the trouble at the mansion?"

"Pulling a circuit breaker and opening a cage wouldn't be too tough for a smart girl like her," Frank said.

"Do you want to question her?" Callie asked.

"Maybe later," Joe replied. "Right now we need to collect some clues of our own."

They moved quickly through the town and across the river to the Book Bank. Chet and Iola were bustling around the store helping out, while Daphne and her mom manned the cash registers and dealt with contest issues.

"You should have picked up a few clues on the way here," Chet said.

"What can we say?" Joe replied, giving Iola a quick hug. "We're foolishly loyal to our friends."

"And we appreciate it!" Daphne called from across the room.

"Not everyone is so gallant," Iola noted. "We had customers already lined up for their free clues at midnight. All the stores up and down the street did, too."

"Which is just what the Chamber of Commerce wanted," Ms. Soesbee added as she bustled by with another pile of clue envelopes.

"Anyone we know among the early birds?" Frank asked Iola.

"Not here," Iola said, "but I saw Missy Gates across the street. And Ren Takei stopped in about ten past."

"He couldn't have gotten here that quickly," Joe said. "Unless he had a head start, that is."

Frank nodded. "There was no law against leaving the party a little early, though."

"Unless it's to cause trouble," Callie added.

"What trouble?" Iola, Chet, Daphne, and her mom said simultaneously. The bookstore fell silent for a moment.

"Probably just a bad circuit breaker," Frank replied. "It shorted out all the lights in the mansion just before midnight."

Ms. Soesbee looked worried. "Oh dear," she said, "I hope it didn't ruin the kickoff."

"Not really," Callie said. "It just made the whole thing spookier."

"Oh, good," Ms. Soesbee said. "A little publicity about a spooky start couldn't hurt things too much."

Frank rubbed his chin. "That's one way of looking at it," he replied. He and Joe exchanged contemplative glances.

"You better get going if you want some clues from other places," Daphne said. "All the merchants are committed to shutting their doors promptly at one A.M."

Joe, Frank, and Callie got in the short line at the register and collected their clue envelopes. Daphne put their names down in the clue register—to prevent them from being able to come back to the store again that night—and the three friends hit the street once more as they opened their envelopes.

"My clue and Joe's are the same!" Callie said, disappointed.

"The distribution is random," Frank said, "so that's not too surprising."

"It wouldn't be a fair contest if you gained too much advantage by teaming up," Joe said.

Callie read the clue out loud. *"Turn, turn while you burn. Some monsters never learn."* She crinkled her pretty nose. "What do you think *that* means?"

"I think it means we need more clues," Joe said. "What does yours say, Frank?"

"It says, *In olden days, he kept his mummies under wraps. Ask, and you shall receive.*"

"These are confusing!" Callie said.

"If they weren't," Frank replied, "it wouldn't be much of a contest. The clues are intentionally obtuse, and most of them just lead to other pieces of the bigger puzzle."

"The mummy thing could be a reference to the pharaohs," Joe said. "Didn't there used to be an Egyptian-style obelisk down at the riverfront park?"

"Yeah, but they moved it to the Bayport museum," Frank replied.

"I dunno, guys," Callie said. "That seems like a pretty weak lead. I'm with Joe—we need more clues."

Frank nodded. "No sense running around on every hunch we've got," he said. "Though I'm sure some people are following that strategy."

"Some *losers*," Callie said, smiling.

"Let's hit some more shops," Joe suggested.

They visited a restaurant down the street from the Book Bank and garnered three more clues. One was a repeat of the mummy hint, and two more concerned bats and crocodiles, and didn't make any more sense than the clues they already had.

"Daphne and her mom sure did a good job on these puzzles," Callie said.

A stop to Pierce's Hardware yielded an instant winner clue for a free cup of coffee at Java John's, a repeat of a clue they already had, and a cryptic message about dragons.

"Just sorting these out from each other is part of the trick," Frank said. "There's no obvious hints of which clues may be connected to each other."

They headed for the north side of the riverfront park, to cross the footbridge into the heart of downtown. As they neared the park, though, Allison Rosenberg shot past them on a bicycle.

"Where'd she get the bike?" Callie asked.

"She probably had it parked somewhere when we saw her running around earlier," Joe said. "Zipping through town on a bike is a good plan."

"If she doesn't get her witch costume caught in the spokes," Frank said.

Allison's Halloween bag full of clues flapped behind her as she wove between two buildings onto Perrin Avenue and toward the bridge. She slowed down as she neared the turn into the park.

Suddenly, a masked figure dressed in jeans, a dark shirt, black cape, and a devil's mask darted out of an alley between the buildings—and grabbed Allison's clue bag.

4 Race with the Devil

Allison skidded wildly as her Halloween bag jerked tight across her chest. She and the bike crashed to the street, and the bag's contents flew into the air. Allison gasped in pain.

Joe and Frank sprinted after the mugger.

"Hey you!" Joe called. "Stop!"

The bandit stopped, but only long enough to scoop up a few of the spilled envelopes. The black-robed devil then turned and ran into the alley across the street.

"Look after Allison," Frank called to Callie. "We'll catch the thief."

Callie Shaw ran to where Allison had fallen. "I'm all right," the girl in the witch costume said, "just a bit shaken up." She and Callie lifted the bike and began to pick up the spilled clues.

Frank and Joe charged into the alley after the bandit. "Any idea who we're chasing?" Joe asked.

"Between the darkness and the mask, who knows?" Frank replied.

The devil-masked thief had a good head start, but the Hardys soon began to close the gap between them.

The thief kept to the alleys, darting pell-mell across the streets in between. Once, a passing car nearly flattened him, but he didn't even look back. The Hardys bolted across just behind the car, hot on his heels.

The bandit turned. He smashed two trash cans at the curb into each other and sent them tumbling across the alleyway.

Frank leaped over the first can, but it rolled into Joe and sent the younger Hardy to the pavement. Frank paused momentarily to make sure his brother was okay. Joe pounded his fist on the ground.

"Don't worry about me," he said. "Catch that guy!"

The dark-haired Hardy nodded and resumed the chase.

The diversion had gained the bandit a good fifteen-yard lead. He crossed the next street—but Frank sprinted out after him.

Headlights flared and a big engine roared as a car barreled straight toward the elder Hardy. The driver of the car leaned hard on the horn and the vehicle's tires squealed.

Frank skidded to a halt, slowing down just enough that the car didn't run him over. He crashed hard into the side of the custom-painted T-bird and the air rushed out of his lungs. Frank fell backward as, across the road, the devil-masked bandit vanished into another alley.

"Frank! Are you all right?" Joe asked, rushing up to his brother.

"I'm okay," Frank said, staggering to his feet. "Just got the wind knocked out of me."

"Why don't you watch where you're going!" called the car's driver. Joe and Frank recognized the face of the sandy-haired teen behind the wheel.

"Harley Bettis," Joe said, "funny finding you here."

"What's so funny about it?" Bettis said, getting out of the car. "I could have killed you!"

"But you didn't," Frank said, brushing himself off. "Thanks."

Bettis fumed. "Don't thank me," he said. He stopped to examine the car where Frank had crashed into it. He rubbed the finish on the red and yellow flames emblazoned on the side. "If this paint job is scratched," he said, "you're paying for it."

"Is this your car?" Joe asked.

"No," Bettis said angrily. "My boss is fixing it up. I was taking it for a test drive. This wasn't my fault, you know."

"No one said it was," Frank replied. "Funny taking a test drive in the middle of the night, though."

Bettis's eyes narrowed. "Everyone's working late because of the contest," he said. "Funny running out of an alley in the middle of the night."

"We were chasing a purse snatcher," Joe said. "Thanks to you, he got away."

"That ain't my fault, either."

"Yeah, we know," Joe said. "Where are you working now, Howard?"

"As if you care," Bettis replied. "I'm at Magnum American Motors, just down the street. Check with my boss if you don't believe me."

"Magnum Motors is giving away one of the big prizes, aren't they?" Frank asked.

"The Geronimo motorcycle," Bettis said. "I'd be trying to win it myself if I weren't disqualified for working there." He stopped fussing over the car's paint job. "Well, there don't seem to be any damage—my boss'll be calling you if there is, though. I gotta get back to work.

"Oh—and keep out of my way. Next time, I might not stop when one of you runs in front of my car—specially if you call me 'Howard' again." Bettis got back into the fiery T-bird and drove away.

"I don't trust that guy," Joe said as the car's taillights disappeared into the darkness. "It's awfully convenient, him showing up just when he did—especially with his friends Missy Gates and Jay

Stone prowling around the contest. This kind of scam is right up their alley."

"Harley's been keeping a pretty low profile since he got in trouble with the juvenile authorities last year, though," Frank said. "And Magnum Motors isn't too far from here."

"Just because he's got a reasonable explanation for being here doesn't mean he wasn't in on this," Joe said. "Snatch-and-grab criminals often have one person to do the crime and another to distract the victims."

Frank nodded. "You could be right. But, speaking of victims, we better see how Allison and Callie are doing."

In a few minutes the brothers retraced their steps to where they'd left the girls.

Callie had called the police on her cell phone while the boys were gone, and one of the downtown cops—Officer Sullivan—had already arrived on the scene.

"Frank, Joe," Callie said, "did you catch him?"

Frank shook his head. "Nope. A car cut us off and we lost him."

"A car driven by Howard 'Harley' Bettis," Joe said.

"Honestly," Allison said to the officer, "there's no need to make a big fuss. It was probably just a prank. Can I get going, please?"

"It's your own business if you don't want to file

charges," Officer Sullivan replied, "but I'd advise you to put in a report."

"Over a couple of slips of paper?" Allison said.

"You might have been hurt," Callie said. "And it's too late to do any more prize hunting tonight, anyway."

Allison checked her watch and frowned. "Well, okay," she said. "But I have to get back home soon. We have school tomorrow, you know."

"I won't keep you long," Officer Sullivan replied. "You Hardy boys should come along and fill out witness statements."

"Yeah, okay," Frank said.

They put Allison's battered bike into the rear of the patrol car and went to the police station.

When they arrived at their homes, just after two A.M., all of them were too tired to worry about either the contest or the devil-masked bandit.

The next day, Bayport High buzzed with talk about the contest. Vice Principal Fazzio patrolled the halls, keeping disruption of classes to a minimum. Enthusiasm spilled over, though, into the study halls, the lunchroom, and classrooms.

" . . . *He kept his mummies under wraps . . .*" Joe said, wondering about one of the clues they'd found last night. He stabbed absentmindedly at his chicken tetrazzini and glanced at Frank and Callie. "I don't get it." Iola, Chet, and Daphne, who were eating across the table from him, merely smiled and kept quiet.

Carrying her empty tray back toward the kitchen, Allison Rosenberg paused a moment. "Are you guys still chasing that mummy clue?" she asked.

"Without much luck, I'm afraid," Frank said.

"Late nights, contest puzzles, and school don't mix too well," Callie added, rubbing her blond head wearily.

Allison smiled and shrugged. "I went to Pierce's Hardware and collected the mummy prize already. I solved the riddle last night, a half hour before I . . . ran into you."

Joe looked puzzled. "So, what did it mean?"

"Jack *Pierce* was the man who did the makeup for the original Universal mummy movies," Allison said. "He kept them under wraps—get it? 'Ask and you shall receive' . . . So I went to Pierce's Hardware, showed the clue, and asked for the loot."

"Was it a good prize?" Joe asked.

"An MP3 player," Allison replied.

"Ren Takei will be jealous," Frank said.

Allison smiled. "He *was.* I showed it to him just before second class. Thanks for helping me out last night, by the way. Don't think I'll cut you any slack in the contest, though."

"We wouldn't want any unfair advantage," Joe replied. "Just ask Iola, Chet, and Daphne."

"Our lips are sealed," Chet said, "even though

Iola and I don't know anything about the riddles."
Daphne merely smiled.

The clue-gathering didn't start again until after dark that evening, which gave the teens plenty of time to finish their homework and other after-school activities.

Iola and Callie worked on their parade float, in the old warehouse down by the docks. Then they met Chet, Daphne, and the Hardys for that evening's hunt.

"Bicycles tonight?" Callie asked.

Joe shook his head. "We'll stick with the van. It'd be easier to get separated on bikes."

"And, given yesterday's events," Frank said, "I think we want to stick together."

They parked the van near the riverfront, in a central location amid the participating stores, then hiked up to the Book Bank to pick up their first clues of the day. Tonight, none of them wore costumes.

On their way into the store, they ran into Ren Takei, who was on his way out. They greeted him, but Ren merely nodded and kept going.

"Think he's ticked about Allison getting that prize?" Joe asked.

"Could be," Frank replied. "Or he could just be concentrating on the contest."

"He's always seemed a little aloof to me," Callie added.

Callie, Frank, and Joe picked up three new clues from Ms. Soesbee, said good-bye to Iola, Chet, and Daphne, then headed down the street to visit more businesses.

"Another duplicate," Joe said, examining the envelopes, "and another crocodile riddle."

"And a free soda at the Town Spa Pizzeria," Callie added.

"We can redeem that when we go downtown later," Frank said.

They stopped at the CD Crate and Lewton Video, picking up two more small food prizes, an instant CD winner, and three duplicates of clues they already had.

"Clearly, the distribution is heavy on the basic clues and small prizes," Frank said.

"They'd go broke if it weren't," Joe replied. "And, besides, I think they want us to use our *brains* on these puzzles as much as our *legs* in collecting them."

"Well, at least we won't go hungry tonight. Kool Kone is nearby. Let's redeem one of those food prizes and pick up some more clues there."

The contest's expanded hours—between dark and midnight—left them a lot of time to collect clues. But with the bustle of people downtown, which seemed to have increased from the previous night, it was slow-going.

"You know," Joe said as he munched a clam roll,

"I've been thinking about the dragon clue we got last night: *Dragons wild may run amok, but near the wall they bring good luck*. I think it's a reference to China. Dragons are lucky there."

"Good thinking, Joe," Frank said. "Isn't there a diorama of the Great Wall in Sui Wing's Chinese restaurant?"

"You're right!" Callie said. "Let's go check it out."

They hiked back over the river, to Sui Wing's restaurant. They greeted the owner, a longtime friend of the Hardys' parents, and then walked over to the Great Wall diorama.

Looking carefully, they spotted a tiny soldier standing under a gate in one of the walls. The banner he held was decorated with a smiling jack-o'-lantern. Callie brought Sui Wing over, and showed him their clue. Mr. Wing reached into the pocket of his chef's apron and produced a piece of paper tied with a green ribbon. "Good luck," he said.

The teens thanked him and then went outside to examine their new clue.

Joe read it aloud. "*Where Boris met his first demise, he found a blade that cut the skies*."

Callie crinkled her nose. "I hope these get easier soon," she said.

"I wouldn't count on it," Frank replied. "I've been thinking about the clue Allison solved earlier, though. It would make sense that most of these puzzles would have a Halloween or horror movie theme. That could help us put the clues together."

"Too bad Chet can't join us," Callie said. "He's a real horror movie buff."

"We'll just have to make do," Joe said. "Do you think you've got something, Frank?"

"Yeah," the elder Hardy replied. "These two clues—*Turn, turn while you burn. Some monsters never learn,* and *Where Boris met his first demise, he found a blade that cut the skies*—could both refer to the original Frankenstein movie, with Boris Karloff?"

"You're right!" Joe said. "The monster gets killed in a windmill at the end of the picture. It was Boris's first big role."

"How does that lead us to another clue?" Callie asked.

"It doesn't," Frank said, "unless you know something about Karloff, and about Bayport's history. Karloff's original name was Pratt."

Joe snapped his fingers. "And Pratt's Antiques on Eagle Hill has an old Dutch windmill on the property!"

"Pratt's has been shut down for years," Callie said. "It would make an ideal place to hide a clue. What are we waiting for? Let's go!"

The three ran back to the van and sped up to the old store. Pratt's Antiques stood near the crest of Eagle Hill, west of town. The shop had closed years ago, but the structure still stood. The road leading to the shop snaked around the hill ending in a weed-covered parking lot.

The old windmill had been brought from Holland by Don Pratt during the business's heyday. Now the windmill stood like a silent sentinel overlooking the abandoned property. Like everything else at Pratt's, the windmill was in shabby repair, almost falling down.

"It looks dangerous," Callie said as they got out of the van.

"It can't be that bad," Joe replied, "or they wouldn't be using it in the contest."

"The city repossessed the property years ago," Frank said. "There's been talk about developing it, but nothing's happened so far." He looked around. "Do you guys see any sign of a clue?"

Callie shook her head. "Maybe it's inside the windmill."

"Good idea," Frank said. Both he and Joe headed for the windmill's battered doorway, with Callie following close behind.

As they approached, though, the huge windmill blades suddenly spun toward the startled teens.

5 Slashing Blades

The windmill blades swooped down. Though the sails were tattered and their wooden ribs gray with age, they were still heavy enough to crack a skull.

"Look out!" Joe called.

He ducked in through the doorway of the old mill as Frank pulled Callie back out of the way. All of them sprawled onto the ground as the blades of the windmill swung between them.

"Why did that happen?" Callie asked, watching the blades as they slowed down once more. "This place has been out of commission for years."

"The only reason it'd happen," Frank said, "is if someone *made* it happen."

Joe glanced up and saw a fleeting shadow. "There's someone in the mill upstairs. C'mon, Frank!"

45

Frank ducked under the slowly moving blade and ran after his brother up the stairs. Callie followed.

The rickety stairs barely held together under the weight of Frank, Joe, and Callie's steps. The windmill tower had several floors, including one with massive, half-rotten, wooden gears. A rope attached to one gave a clue as to how the ancient blades had sprung to life.

"He must have pulled that rope to spin the blades," Joe said.

"A pity his aim wasn't better," Frank said with a grim smile. "A pity for *him*."

A wooden ladder in the middle of the second landing led up through a trapdoor onto the third floor. Before they could reach it, though, someone hauled the ladder up through the hole.

The brothers saw a shadow moving above as they ran to the trapdoor. Frank knitted his fingers together and held his locked hands at knee height.

"*Allez-oop!*" he said.

Joe put his foot in Frank's hands and the elder Hardy thrust his brother up into the hole. Joe climbed halfway up, then dropped back suddenly without warning. He held on to the door by just his fingertips.

Frank gave another shove on Joe's feet, and he surged through the trapdoor. Frank leaped up, grabbed the ledge, and pulled himself after his brother.

As he did this, a shadowy figure jumped out of the room's only window. The prowler grabbed onto an unmoving windmill blade, and slid down a long vane as though it were a firepole.

The ancient blade buckled and cracked under the intruder's weight, and a large piece snapped off just as he hit the ground.

Joe reached the window a moment later and looked as though he might go after the saboteur, but Frank held him back. "A second person trying that stunt would snap that blade," the elder Hardy said.

The intruder raced across the clearing at the windmill's base, and vanished into the woods surrounding the hilltop.

"Are you guys all right up there?" Callie called from below.

"We're fine," Frank called back. "But the culprit got away." As he lowered the ladder to his girlfriend, a motor sprang to life somewhere in the forested hill below the windmill.

"Sounds like he had a motorcycle or four-wheeler stashed nearby," Joe said angrily.

"How'd he escape?" Callie asked, looking around the small room.

"Out the window and down the windmill vane," Frank said, "but it broke when he landed."

"Did you see who it was?" Callie crossed to the window and peered out.

Joe shook his head. "Devil Mask again. He didn't have his cape, though, this time."

"He got the clue," Frank said, picking up pieces of a ceramic pumpkin lying on the floor.

"Not the only clue," Callie said. "Look!"

The brothers joined her at the window and gazed out across the yard of the old antique shop. Written in white paint on the roof of the old building were the words: *Vlad & Van took the trip, but not in their usual seats.*

"The rules said that there would be big clues to the big prizes," Callie noted.

"And that everyone would have a chance to find them," Joe added. "I guess that's because they're too big to steal."

"A good thing, too," Frank said. "Otherwise, Devil Mask would have left us with zip to go on."

"Then maybe it was a prize certificate he got in the ceramic pumpkin, not a clue," Callie said.

"That makes sense," Frank said. "The rules said that putting two or more clues together would lead to some kind of reward. Maybe that could help us figure out who this bandit is."

Joe nodded. "*If* we could discover what prize was in that pumpkin."

"It should be something better than just a free cup of coffee," Callie noted.

Frank ran his fingers through his hair. "It's a start, anyway." He wrote the clue from the rooftop on the same paper as the two clues that had led them to the windmill. "We've got all we can here," he said. "Let's get back to town."

They piled back into the van and headed for downtown once more. As Frank drove, Joe said, "You know, working at Magnum Motors, Harley Bettis has access to motorcycles. And we know the Kings have worked with cars and cycles before."

"Bettis is a pretty athletic guy," Callie added. "He could probably make that jump and slide down the windmill vane."

"But he cut us off in that car the first time we chased Devil Mask," Frank said. "He could be working with one of the other Kings, though. Maybe he, Jay Stone, and Missy Gates are all in this together."

"It wouldn't be the first time," Joe noted.

Midnight was fast approaching by the time the three teens parked the van and got back into the game. They stopped and redeemed their food prizes, picking up more clues and a certificate for a free CD along the way. Most of the clues turned out to be duplicates of ones they already had.

"It's like those fast-food contests where you get a billion of the same pieces, but can't find the one you need to complete a set," Callie noted.

"*Vanderdecken wouldn't be caught undead tying one on here,*" Joe said, reading aloud a clue that they hadn't seen before.

"Sounds like a beer reference," Frank said.

"Doesn't 'tying one on' mean something like 'getting drunk'?"

"Right—but there are no bars or liquor stores in the sponsor list," Callie said. "I'm sure the contest is meant to be family friendly."

"Could Vanderdecken be the same Van as in the antique shop clue?" Joe asked.

"Maybe," Frank replied. "With *Van* and *Vlad*, though, I was thinking it might be Dracula and Van Helsing. The historical Dracula's name was Vlad Tepes."

"Too bad Chet and Daphne are the only horror movie buffs we know," Callie said.

"And Allison Rosenberg, apparently," Frank said.

Callie bit her lip.

"Some Internet searching after the deadline tonight may give us a leg up tomorrow," Joe suggested. "For now, though, we better keep picking up clues."

Other contestants—many in costume—scurried along the darkened streets. The Hardys and their friends also prowled the shops, looking for new clues. They said hello to the people they knew, and occasionally stopped to chat with other clue hunters.

Rumors of sizable wins by a few contestants spread like wildfire through downtown.

"I heard that some guy won a motorbike earlier," Tony Prito said. He was an old friend of the Hardys and worked in a local pizza shop.

"Anyone we know?" Joe asked. "One of the Kings, maybe?"

Tony shrugged. "I don't think so. It wasn't anyone I ever heard of. Allison Rosenberg won a pair of inline skates, though. Ren Takei scored a handheld computer tonight, too."

"Bet that's made him unbearably pleased," Frank said.

"Yeah," Tony said. "He was smiling like the cat that ate the canary."

"I wonder if Allison will be using the skates or her bike from now on," Callie said. "Have you seen her?"

Tony nodded. "She's not in costume tonight," he said. "I think she's playing it safe after the trouble last night—though I did see her earlier today, zipping around on her bike. How are you guys doing?"

"Won some food and a CD," Joe replied. "We found one of the big clues, too—but someone beat us to it. They swiped the prize and we just got another piece of the puzzle."

"Most of this stuff is over my head," Tony admitted. "I'm going for the short, sweet stuff. That's what a lot of the kids are doing." Then he smiled. "The mysteries should be right up your alley, though. Time for me to run. Good luck, guys. I gotta get back to Mr. Pizza and finish up my shift. I'm only here on a break." He hopped on his bike and headed back toward the mall where he worked.

Frank rubbed his chin. "So," he said, "Allison and Takei have both won expensive prizes tonight."

Joe frowned. "Among dozens of others, probably," he said. "I'm thinking that finding the person who took the prize from the antique shop may be impossible."

"Me, too," Callie said. "Let's keep concentrating on the clues. If a lot of folks are going for the short-term prizes, that would still leave us a good chance for the bigger-ticket items. Slow and steady wins the race."

"Let's hope," Frank said.

"I get the feeling that Allison may want it all," Joe said. As he spoke, Allison Rosenberg zipped past on her bicycle. She waved; they waved back.

"Let's get going," said Callie.

They hiked up past the Browning Theater and stopped in at the CD Crate, where they picked up their CD prize and scored a few more clues.

"More crocodiles," Joe said, scratching his blond head. "And this: *Orange, orange all around, carving clues are often found.*"

Frank shrugged. "As much as I hate to admit it, there may be some of these puzzles that we just won't get."

Callie laughed. "The invincible Frank and Joe Hardy admit defeat?"

"Not on your life!" Joe replied.

As they walked back toward the center of town,

Callie spotted a familiar figure at the Kool Kone drive-in restaurant. "I didn't know Brent Jackson drove a motorcycle," she said.

Sure enough, Jackson sat astride a large dirt bike in the Kool Kone parking lot. The mud on the bike's fenders looked fresh.

Anger burned in Joe's eyes, and he strode up to his football rival. "Been doing some off-road driving tonight, Jackson?" he asked.

Brent Jackson regarded the younger Hardy coolly. "What business is it of yours?" he said. He stood and, laying his helmet on the seat of the bike, walked toward the Hardys.

"Some jerk on an off-roader tried to mess with us while we were hunting up clues, that's all," Joe replied.

"He nearly got all three of us," Frank said. "He was wearing a mask, though, so we didn't get a good look at him. Where were you about an hour ago, Brent?"

"You ain't my mother, Hardy," Jackson said. "You want to know where I've been, figure it out on your own. Too bad that guy missed."

"Want a second crack at it, tough guy?" Joe asked, balling up his fists.

"Nope," Jackson replied, turning away. Without warning, he spun back around and threw a punch at Joe's head.

6 Ghost Riders

Brent Jackson grinned as his fist sailed toward Joe's face.

Joe ducked out of the way and Brent's fist merely grazed his shoulder. The younger Hardy counter-punched, but Jackson blocked the blow and threw another jab of his own.

"You've needed your clock cleaned for a long time, Hardy!" Jackson said through gritted teeth.

"Too bad the only thing you've ever cleaned is a plate," Joe replied. He sidestepped the punch and hammered Brent in the ribs.

Jackson staggered back, the air rushing out of his lungs. A crowd began to gather around the fight. About half the kids at the drive-in seemed to be cheering for Jackson, the other half for Joe.

Jackson scrambled to his feet and lunged at Joe. Joe tried to back away, but got pinned against the burgeoning crowd. Jackson buried his shoulder in the younger Hardy's gut, and the two of them tumbled to the ground.

Joe kneed Jackson in the ribs, and rolled out from under him. As the two got to their feet, Frank and Callie stepped in between the boys.

"That's enough!" Frank said.

"This isn't doing anyone any good," Callie added.

The assembled crowd started to boo.

"So, now your brother and his girl do your fighting for you, Hardy?" Jackson said, glaring at Joe.

"Frank, Callie, keep out of this," Joe said, not taking his eyes off Jackson.

"What's all the commotion here?" boomed an authoritative voice.

Everyone turned and saw Officer Sullivan approaching, along with Sean M. Benson, the owner of Kool Kone. Benson was a brawny man, half a head taller than Sullivan, and just as wide. He wore an apron with a Kool Kone logo and a badge with his nickname—"Mike"—on his lapel.

"Nothing, Officer Sullivan," Frank said. "Just a little disagreement over contest rules."

The cop scowled. "Any more disagreements, and you'll all be disagreeing with the chief of police," he said. "Understand?"

Joe and Jackson nodded sullenly.

"I won't have any fighting on my property," Benson said. "Both of you scram. I don't want to see either of you back here again until this contest is over. I don't need troublemakers messing up my business."

"Sorry, Mr. Benson," Joe said.

Jackson put on his motorcycle helmet and sneered at Joe. "That's another one I owe you, Hardy."

"Put it on my account," Joe replied.

As Jackson took off on his bike, Joe, Frank, and Callie walked down the street away from Kool Kone.

Joe frowned. "I feel like a real jerk," he said.

"You could have picked a better time and place to fight, that's for sure," Frank said.

"But the way Jackson talked, it made me feel *sure* that he was the one that made all the trouble up at Pratt's Antiques."

"It seems to me," Callie said, "that Jackson's *always* like that—at least when it comes to you and Frank."

"Yeah," Joe said. "Maybe. He better stay out of my way until the contest is over, though."

"We should probably try to stay out of his way as well," Frank said. "We won't be winning any contests inside police HQ."

As they walked, the clock in St. Patrick's Church struck midnight. The game was officially over for the day.

"Let's get home," Callie said. "There's nothing more we can do tonight."

As they hiked back to the van, they noticed other contestants still running around town—Allison Rosenberg, Missy Gates, Jay Stone, and Ren Takei among them.

"They must be following up clues," Frank said.

"Too bad I feel pretty clueless at the moment," Joe replied.

"It'll all look better after a good night's sleep, I'm sure," Callie said.

Joe sighed. "Let's hope Allison and Ren leave *some* clues for us to solve."

Chores and homework left the brothers little time to think about the contest until after school the next day.

They were slightly dismayed to hear that someone had solved the crocodile series of puzzles, and claimed a boat as a reward. "The newspaper has started announcing when the big prizes are won— so people won't waste too much time working on puzzles that are already solved," Chet said, as he walked home from school with the Hardys.

"So, what was the crocodile riddle about?" Joe asked.

"You'll have to check the paper," Chet said. "My lips are sealed." He motioned as though he were zippering them.

"Who won?" Frank asked.

"Someone named Julie Kendall," Chet replied.

"No one we know," Joe said. "We've got a lot of competition in this."

"And not nearly enough information to go on," Frank added.

"Keep plugging," Chet said. "I'm sure you'll solve one of the puzzles, sooner or later. See you at the shop tonight."

"Sure thing," Joe replied.

He and Frank stopped at home to complete their homework and have a snack. Then they went to the old dockside warehouse to pick up the girls.

Callie and Iola, along with the rest of the float committee, were working in the huge storage building that had once been the pride of Bayport's fishing industry. Now long abandoned, it was little more than the city's largest garage, though a few rooms on the north side were still filled with old nautical equipment.

Floats for the upcoming Halloween parade filled the big room. All had spooky themes, and many were funny, too. Callie and Iola's project was called the "Werewolf's Wagon." It looked like something out of a 1960s hot-rod model kit. Not to be outdone, another group had patched together a car called "Dracula's Dragster."

"This should be some *spooktacular* race to the parade finish line," Joe said, climbing behind the wheel of the wolf car.

Iola laughed. "I wouldn't count on winning too

much with either of these two," she said. "They may look pretty good on the outside, but they're held together with chewing gum."

Joe smiled at her. "Maybe you and I should take the Werewolf's Wagon for a moonlight ride."

"I have it on good authority," Callie said, "that come midnight, that hot rod turns into a pumpkin."

"Or a lemon, maybe," Frank added with a grin.

"So," Iola said, "you two detectives figured out who's behind that devil mask yet?"

"Brent Jackson's still my top candidate," Joe said. "He's jerk enough to make all this trouble."

"If he's won a prize yet, though, we haven't heard about it," Callie said.

"He might not claim the prize right away," Frank noted. "That would be a good way to ward off suspicion. I'm not sure about him, though. Harley Bettis is pretty high on my list."

"If either of them were brainier, they'd be better bets," Joe said. "As it is . . ." He shrugged.

"Bettis does have the Kings to back him up," Callie pointed out.

"That's why I'm thinking we should do a little more checking on him tonight," Frank said. "After we drop Iola off at the Book Bank, I mean."

"We could scout out where he works," Joe added. "Magnum Motors isn't too far away from the Soesbees' store—and pretty close to where he kept us from catching the devil-masked man the other day."

"Do you think the devil-masked man could be a woman?" Callie asked. "Missy Gates is pretty spry, after all."

"It's possible," Frank said. "The only way we'll find out is to keep working on the case."

"We better head to the shop then," Iola said. "It's nearly dark already."

They all piled into the Hardys' van and drove to the Book Bank. They arrived just as Chet walked in with the night's supply of carry-out food; the frenzy of the contest had left the Soesbees and the Mortons with little time for dinner breaks.

The store bustled with customers, even before the official beginning of the night's contest. Some were waiting for dusk and the start of the Spooktacular, while others were just regular shoppers.

Councilwoman Hamilton stood in one corner, talking animatedly to Kathryn Soesbee. None of the friends could hear what the women were saying.

"What's up with that?" Joe asked Daphne.

"Just some contest business," Daphne replied. "The councilwoman's always on edge—which doesn't help Mom's mood, either."

"I thought the contest had been going well," Frank said.

"Oh yeah," Daphne said. "Real well. But real crazy, too. Did you hear that some contestants nearly got into a fight down at Kool Kone last night?"

"We hadn't heard that," Joe managed to say with a straight face.

Darkness fell, and the streets of Bayport swarmed with costumed treasure hunters once more.

The Hardys and Callie picked up their traditional first clues of the night at the Book Bank, then they hopped in the van and drove over to Magnum American Motors. They'd decided to use the car for some stops tonight—at least until they got back over the river, into the city's center.

Magnum American Motors was a large blue-and-gray cinder block building on top of a bluff that was just a few blocks from the riverbank. The building had a big picture window in front, with neon motorcycle logos hanging from the corners. A beautiful red, white, and blue chopper dominated the display. A sign in the corner by the bike's back wheel proclaimed, "Proud Sponsor of the Bayport Spooktacular!"

"That must be the limited edition Geronimo they're giving away," Frank noted.

Joe let out a low whistle. "She sure is a beaut."

"I wouldn't mind winning it," Callie said. "Though I suppose I'd have to share it with you two weirdos."

Frank gave his girlfriend a quick hug. "I'm sure we could work out a timeshare or something," he said.

"We'll have to win it, first," Joe said.

A chime above the door rang as they entered the

dealership. Inside, motorcycles, snowmobiles, and four-wheelers dominated the display floor. Nearly all the brands displayed were high end, and every one was an American-made model.

On the left side of the room there was a service counter; a small office stood on the right. A corridor between the two led to the garage in the back of the building, the rest rooms, and the rear alleyway exit.

Harley Bettis prowled behind the parts counter, polishing the top with a dirty rag. He wore an oil-stained gray jumpsuit and looked very much at home amid the machine parts. He looked up and scowled as the teens entered.

"What do you want?" he asked.

"We just came in to look around," Joe said, "and maybe pick up a few clues."

"The boss handles the clues," Bettis said.

"Well, could we see him, then?" Callie asked.

"I'll get him," Bettis said. He turned toward the back of the shop, then turned around and said, "Don't be making any trouble here. This is my job, you know."

"We'll stay out of the way," Frank said with a friendly smile.

Bettis nodded suspiciously, and slunk between two of the long parts shelves. He went through a door at the back of the room and into the garage.

"Friendly sales staff," Joe said sarcastically.

"He's certainly acting like he has something to hide," Callie noted.

A moment later a burly man with curly hair and a bushy mustache walked up the corridor between the office and the parts counter. He smiled and wiped his hands on a clean rag. "Sorry about that," he said. "I was just working in back. This is a busy time, you know."

The teens didn't see anyone else in the dealership, but they didn't say anything.

The man extended his hand. "I'm Rod Magnum," he said, "owner of Magnum American Motors. How can I help you tonight?"

Frank shook his hand.

"I'm Frank Hardy. This is my brother Joe, and my girlfriend, Callie Shaw. We just came in to check the place out and gather our free clues."

Magnum nodded knowingly.

"Is that the cycle you're giving away?" Joe asked, tilting his head toward the motorcycle in the front window.

"That's her," Magnum said. "Isn't she a beaut? Limited edition. Someone'll be pretty lucky to win her." He walked behind the sales counter, brought out a big jar full of clue envelopes, and held it out to the teens. "Take your pick."

The phone rang. Bettis, returning from the garage, said, "I got it." He talked quietly into the phone, and turned his back on the others.

The Hardys and Callie picked three clues out of the jar while keeping an eye on Bettis.

"Thanks very much," Frank said. "We'll have to come down here and shop around after the contest is over."

"Shop around now, if you like," Magnum said. "I've got time."

"We have to be getting back to the contest," Callie replied.

Bettis put down the phone. "I'm going on break," he said.

Magnum looked at him and frowned. "Don't take too long," he said. "Business will pick up any minute now."

Bettis nodded.

"Thanks again, Mr. Magnum," Joe said, shaking Magnum's hand.

"Tell all your friends," Magnum said, "only the best at Magnum American Motors."

After the three teenagers exited the store, Callie said, "Bettis is definitely up to something. Did you see how suspiciously he acted when he got that phone call?"

"Maybe we should see where he's headed," Joe suggested.

They all got into the van. Joe pulled around to the alley just in time to see Bettis leaving on a beat-up old motorcycle.

"That could be the one he used to escape from the windmill last night," Callie said.

"Maybe," Frank said. "Try not to let him see us, Joe."

Joe chuckled. "As if I don't know how to tail someone."

Bettis kept to the alleyways as he headed toward the edge of downtown. Joe circled the blocks, keeping the van out of the alleys in order to avoid being spotted. It was a tricky maneuver, but the younger Hardy was pulling it off without a hitch. That is, until they circled a block where Bettis didn't come out.

"He must have stopped somewhere in there," Frank said. "Pull over. We'll have to look for him on foot."

Joe found a parking spot, and the three of them quickly backtracked on foot to where they'd last seen Bettis.

As they crept between the garages and back entrances of stores, they heard Bettis's threatening voice.

"If you try to ruin this setup," Bettis said, "I'll break your neck."

7 The Shuttered Store

"Can you see him? Who's he threatening?" Callie whispered.

Joe and Frank peered into the alleyway, but they couldn't see their quarry. They shrugged.

"We'll have to sneak closer," Frank whispered.

The three of them moved toward Bettis's voice, carefully avoiding the trash cans and other obstacles in their way.

"I mean it," Bettis said, his voice echoing through the alley. "If you screw this up for me, I'll make you regret it. Big time."

A muffled voice drifted back to the three friends, but they couldn't make out what it was saying.

"I don't care what you do," Bettis said, "just as long as you keep me out of it. I've got my own fish to fry here. And if you get in my way . . ." He let the threat hang in the air for a moment before continuing. "I've worked long and hard to get here, and I'm not gonna let some half-baked scheme foul it up."

The Hardys and Callie crept closer. Peering around a garage and a Dumpster, they saw Bettis with a person in a bulky motorcycle jacket and helmet. The two stood in the shadows between two buildings. The helmeted person was facing away from the brothers. Bettis looked angry.

"You've been warned," Bettis said. "Keep your nose out of it—*way* out of it. I'll make you regret it if you don't."

A muffled laugh came from the helmet.

Bettis's eyes narrowed.

"Someone's watching us!" he said. "Take off—I don't want to be seen with you." He pulled his helmet onto his head, and he and his cohort fired up their motorcycles.

"They've spotted us!" Joe whispered.

"Back to the van," Frank said. "Maybe we can follow them."

The Hardys and Callie ran back toward the van as Bettis and the other cyclist took off. Bettis went up the alley, away from the brothers, and the other person darted down the small walkway between two buildings.

"Rats!" Callie said as they reached the van. "There's

no way we can catch whoever Bettis was talking to."

"Maybe Bettis will lead us to some more info, then," Frank said. He hopped behind the wheel and started the van while the other two climbed in.

Bettis had a good head start on them, but Frank knew the Bayport roads, and a trick or two about tailing as well. In less than a minute, he had Bettis's taillights in sight once more.

"He won't spot us if I hang back," Frank said.

"Why don't you turn off the lights?" Callie said. "Bettis would never see us then."

Frank shook his head. "Too dangerous with all these contestants milling around," he replied. "The streets are a lot more crowded than usual."

"We wouldn't want to clobber anyone the way Bettis nearly clobbered us the other night," Joe added.

"Who do you think Bettis was talking to?" Callie asked.

"My guess is either Jay Stone or Missy Gates," Joe said. "It sounded like he didn't want them horning in on whatever scheme he's got up his sleeve."

"If Bettis has gone out on his own, the rest of the Kings gang can't be too happy about it," Frank said. "They probably want to get in on his action."

"I'm surprised the juvenile authorities let Bettis off so light," Callie said. "They should have locked him up for good."

"Well, maybe he'll be nailed with some harsher punishment this time," Joe replied.

When it looked as though Bettis might turn back and see them, Frank took a couple of quick turns. "He doesn't look like he's going anywhere in particular," Frank said. "He's just winding around through the back streets."

"Maybe he's trying to shake us off," Joe suggested.

"Yeah." Frank smiled. "Too bad it won't work. I'll stay back a bit farther, and give him enough rope to hang himself."

They trailed behind Bettis for another five minutes, keeping well out of sight. Gradually the motorcycle rider stopped dodging through the alleys and side streets.

"I hate to say this, guys," Callie said, "but it looks like he may be heading back to Magnum Motors."

Joe frowned and checked his watch. "He's been gone about twenty minutes," Joe said. "It's a long break—but not *too* long. I have a feeling Callie's right."

Frank rapped his palm on the steering wheel. "If only we could have followed the other rider," he said.

"We did everything we could," Joe said. "At least we know that Bettis is up to something—even if we don't know *what*."

"We've seen three people on motorcycles," Callie said. "Any one of them could have been at Pratt's Antiques last night."

Bettis turned up Racine Street and went past the

Book Bank before turning east toward Magnum Motors. Frank slowed the van down. "No use following him any further," he said.

"Who's that hanging out in front of the Book Bank?" Callie asked.

"And why is the store dark?" Joe added.

Frank pulled the van into the nearest available spot. All three of them got out and moved quickly up the street toward the Book Bank.

No lights were coming from the interior of the store. A man in a trench coat and hat moved cautiously around the storefront, peering into the windows and glancing around apprehensively. In the dark, none of them could make out the man's face.

Spotting the brothers and Callie advancing toward him, the man pulled his hat lower and turned to leave.

"Stop right there!" Joe called. "What are you doing?"

The man kept walking.

The Hardys broke into a sprint. "Callie, call the police," Frank said.

The man turned as they approached. "No, please," he said. "No police. I wasn't doing anything untoward."

"Mr. Blasko?" Callie asked. She peered into the darkness, her fingers paused over the keys of her cell phone.

"Why is the store dark?" Joe asked.

"I'm sure that I don't know," Blasko said, taking off his hat and bowing slightly to Callie. He looked strange and ghostly in the pale light from the distant streetlamps. "I found it this way moments ago."

"What are you doing here?" Callie asked.

"I was stopping by for a bit of light reading—I haven't been sleeping well. Odd that they should be closed during the contest, don't you think?"

Frank nodded, his eyes narrowing as he regarded the aging horror movie star. "Yes," Frank said, "very odd."

"Well," Blasko said, "I must be going."

"What's your hurry?" Joe asked.

"No hurry," the movie star replied, "but it is late, and I'm tired. Could you direct me to another bookstore, by any chance?"

"I think there's a Denning and Hayday open late near the mall," Callie said. "You'd have to take a cab out there, though. Do you want me to call one?"

Blasko shook his head. "No. No. It sounds like entirely too much trouble. I'll just have to make do, I suppose."

"Would you like us to drop you at your hotel?" Frank asked.

"Don't bother," Blasko replied. "I can find my own way. Walking is good for the constitution, you know." He turned and strolled away.

"That's funny," Joe said when Blasko had walked

out of earshot, "he was going to leave the opposite way when we first confronted him."

"Maybe he thought we were muggers or something," Callie said. "We did come up on him all of a sudden."

"Maybe," Frank said, rubbing his chin, "but that story of his just doesn't ring true to me."

"Do you want to follow him?" Joe asked.

"We'd better see what's going on here, first," Frank said.

He peered through the window of the Book Bank and saw a small emergency light burning way in the back—near the rear exit.

"Where do you think they are?" Joe asked.

Frank shrugged and tried the door. "It's not locked," he said, swinging the door inward. He and Joe got out their pocket flashlights.

"Ms. Soesbee? Daphne? Iola? Chet?" Frank called. "Anybody here?"

There was no answer.

They shone their flashlights around the store's interior.

"Everything looks normal," Joe said, "aside from the fact that the place is dark and deserted."

"Where could they all have gone?" Callie said.

"Maybe the circuit breaker blew," Frank suggested.

"It's in the back, probably," Joe replied. "Let's check and see if we can get the lights on."

The three of them moved cautiously through the shadowy bookshelves, toward the back of the store.

"This place sure is creepy with the lights out," Callie said.

"I think this could have been another attempt to add some 'atmosphere' to the treasure hunt," Frank replied.

"This is *not* atmosphere," Joe said. "Look!"

He shone his light into the ancient bank vault near the back of the store. The vault's door stood open. Jumbled papers covered the room's floor.

"That's where they keep the game clues, isn't it?" Callie asked.

"We better check it out," Joe said. Then, in a lower voice, he added, "There might be someone inside."

Moving silently, the Hardys and Callie crept forward into the old vault. Frank crouched into a martial-arts stalking position. Joe followed, after handing his flashlight to Callie.

When they entered the old room, though, they found only more scattered papers.

"No one's here," Frank said.

Callie let out a sigh of relief. "What a mess!" she said.

As the words left her lips, the door of the old bank vault slammed shut behind them—trapping the Hardys and Callie inside.

8 Vault of Horror

Joe pounded on the door with his fist.

"Who's out there?" he called. "Let us out!"

"If that's you, Chet, this isn't funny!" Callie added.

Frank shook his head. "This isn't Chet's style."

"Let us out!" Joe said, pounding again.

"Save your breath, Joe," Frank said. "Whoever shut that door is probably gone."

Callie looked around nervously. The only light in the room came from the flashlight in her hand, and from the tiny, barred window set high in one wall. "How soon do you think the air will run out?" she asked.

"Not before morning at the earliest," Frank replied. "We could probably stay in here for days if we smash that little window."

"Let's do it, then," Joe said.

"Hold on," said Frank. "Let's not break things if we don't have to. Chances are pretty good that someone will come back to the store soon and let us out."

"What about breaking down the door?" Callie suggested.

Frank shook his head. "The bolt on the other side is inch–thick steel. We'd only hurt ourselves trying to break through."

Joe pulled out the Hardys' cell phone and dialed; Callie did the same with hers.

"Nothing," she said, frowning. "No service."

"Probably because we're inside a metal vault," Frank concluded.

"Man, I hate waiting to be rescued," Joe said, pacing around the small chamber.

"It could be worse," Frank replied. "We've got a little light, even without the flashlights—and plenty of air. At the worst, we'll just spend an uncomfortable night here. Our parents are bound to find us in the morning, if not sooner."

"Do you think Bettis could have rushed back here and locked us in?" Joe asked.

"I don't see how," Frank said. "The store was already dark when we were following him. Whatever occurred here happened before then."

"He could have had an accomplice," Joe said. "We already know he's working with someone—the guy he threatened. It's not a big stretch to think he set us up."

"Mr. Blasko might have done it, too," Callie said. "We don't know how long he'd been here when we showed up. Maybe he was coming *out* of the Book Bank when we caught him, and not just looking around. He could have followed us after we came inside, and locked us in."

"It's possible," Frank said. He sat down by the door.

"Where are Chet and the others, though?" Callie asked, sitting down beside him. "Do you think something's happened to them?" She was clearly worried.

"If anything has, there's nothing we can do about it, as long as we're trapped in here," Joe said. He pounded his fist against the door one last time, then sat down amid the piles of papers. He leaned back against the brick wall and took a long, deep breath. "Do you think whoever did this got what he came for?"

"No way to tell," Frank said. "We must have almost caught him, though. Otherwise, why would he lock us in?" He smiled at Callie, then glanced at the flashlight. "We should save the light."

She nodded and turned it off. "I hope the Mortons and the Soesbees are all right," she said.

"I'm sure they're fine," Joe replied. "Chet and Iola are tough, and Daphne's no pushover, either.

There's probably a logical explanation for why they're not here."

"Maybe someone lured them away," Frank suggested, "so he could ransack the place."

"But how?" Callie asked.

"Hey! Listen!" Joe said. "Someone's rummaging around out there." He stood and pounded on the door again. "Hey! Let us out! We're trapped in here!"

Frank stood and positioned himself beside the door, ready to clobber anyone who came through. "Just in case," he whispered to Callie. She came and stood beside him, ready to help. Joe continued to bang on the vault door.

Slowly the door creaked open and light shone in from the bookstore beyond. A face appeared, silhouetted by the light.

"Who's in there? Are you okay?" asked a familiar voice.

"Chet!" Callie said. "Are we glad to see you!"

"Callie, Frank, Joe?" Chet said. "What are you doing in the vault? Did you guys turn off the lights in the store?"

Joe shook his head as he, Frank, and Callie exited the vault. "They were off when we got here," Joe said. "When we came to investigate, someone locked us in."

"Chet, where have you been?" Callie said. "Where are Iola and the Soesbees? We were worried."

"Iola had a headache, so she went home," Chet

said. "Daphne had to pick up some schoolwork; she's been falling behind because of the contest. Her mom had to take care of some contest business with the Chamber of Commerce. They all left together."

"Which means you were left minding the store," Joe said.

Chet nodded. "Yeah. Then the Town Spa Pizzeria called, and said we needed to pick up the carry-out order we'd phoned in. So I stuck the 'Back in Fifteen Minutes' sign on the door and went out to get it." He indicated the pizza boxes on the sales counter.

"You left the lights on and the door locked?" Frank asked.

"Of course," Chet replied. "I was only going to be gone a couple of minutes."

"Whoever turned out the lights must have taken down the sign, too," Joe said.

"They probably didn't want any contest-goers prowling around while they ransacked the vault," Frank said.

"Oh, man!" Chet said. "I was so busy wondering what you guys were doing in there that I didn't notice. What a mess!"

At that moment, the shop's back door opened, and Daphne and her mom entered. Concern flashed over Ms. Soesbee's face. "What's going on here?" she asked.

"I had to go out and pick up the pizzas you

ordered," Chet said. "While I was gone, someone broke in."

Both mother and daughter's jaws dropped open.

"What did they steal?" Ms. Soesbee asked, nearly frantic.

"It doesn't look like they took anything from the store," Frank said. "The vault is a mess, though."

"Oh, no!" Ms. Soesbee said, peering inside at the scattered papers.

"We arrived before the burglar left," Joe said, "but when we went to investigate the vault, he locked us in."

"This is terrible!" Daphne said.

"We should call the police," Callie suggested.

"No!" Ms. Soesbee snapped. "No police. Let's figure out what's missing first. The contest doesn't need the bad publicity that calling the police would bring."

"You said you went out to pick up pizza, Chet?" Daphne said.

"Yeah. The Town Spa Pizzeria called to say it was ready, so I locked up and went to get it. If figured you must have forgotten about the order when you ran out. Sorry. I never would have gone if I'd known the place would get broken into."

"But we didn't order any pizza," Daphne said.

"The pizza must have been a ruse to lure Chet away from the store," Joe said, glancing at the steaming pizza boxes on the counter. "The question is, what was inside the vault that's worth that much trouble?"

"Only the contest materials have been scattered," Ms. Soesbee said. "We'll need to put them back before we can confirm what's missing."

"We can help with that," Callie said. Joe and Frank nodded.

"Thank you so much," Ms. Soesbee replied.

They all went into the vault and collected the scattered clue envelopes. While the others worked, Chet stayed out front and dealt with customers.

In a short time they'd stacked and counted the envelopes that had spilled on the floor. Ms. Soesbee frowned as they brought them back to the corner of the store that served as her office. "They all seem to be here," she said, puzzled. "It doesn't look like anything is missing. Of course, I'll have to recheck the clues before sending them out."

Daphne gave a half smile. "This is as far as you three go, unless you want to work *with* the contest instead of *on* the contest."

"Were all the clues in the vault?" Joe asked.

"All but the ones we've already distributed," Ms. Soesbee replied.

"Why go to all the trouble of breaking in here and not take anything?" Callie asked.

Daphne shrugged. "You can't claim a prize without the proper chain of clue envelopes—so just checking some clues wouldn't do any good."

Frank rubbed his chin. "Well, it might give you some advantage," he said, "but you couldn't cash in on it unless you could obtain the right clue later. That seems like a big chance to take. It would have been easier just to steal the clue you wanted."

"What are the colored dots on the corners of the envelopes for?" Joe asked.

"There's a different color dot for each day of the contest," Ms. Soesbee said. "We put out a different batch of clues each day."

"Clues are easier to understand during the last days," Daphne added.

Frank shook his head. "I don't think there's anything more we can do here—except get ourselves disqualified from competing. I still think you should call the police, though."

"We will, if anything turns up stolen," Ms. Soesbee said. "But maybe this is just someone's idea of a prank." She looked around the store. "There are plenty of valuables out here, in plain sight. A *real* burglar could have taken any of it."

"Picking the front door lock is a lot of trouble to go to for a prank," Joe said.

"Let us know if you find anything gone," Frank said. "Come on, Joe, Callie. We better get back to the contest if we're going to have any chance at the big prizes."

"Good luck," Daphne and Chet said simultaneously. They laughed.

The Hardys and Callie walked in the direction of Java John's, hitting a few stores for clues as they went.

Allison Rosenberg drove by once and beeped at them. She was seated behind the wheel of a classic, orange VW beetle. "Like it?" she called, pulling over. "I just collected it for solving the scarab riddles."

"Congratulations," Frank said.

"I hope this means you're retiring," Joe added.

Allison laughed. "Not on your life." She put her foot on the gas and zipped away.

"I don't think we've even seen the scarab riddles," Callie said.

After an hour they stopped at Java John's to get some drinks and gather their wits.

Callie sipped her mocha latte and read one of their new clues. *"Where blanket boy might meet a most sincere wicked witch,"* she said, then sighed. "These *aren't* getting any easier."

"Hang on," Joe said, "that might tie in with a clue we found yesterday." He hauled it out and read, *"Orange, orange all around, carving clues are often found."*

"How does that fit?" Callie asked.

"Seeing Allison in that VW made me think about a big pumpkin," Joe explained. "Get it? These two riddles could both be about pumpkins."

Callie's eyes brightened. "The boy would be the kid from 'Peanuts' who sat in the pumpkin patch. What about the witch, though?"

"Maybe it's a location of some kind," Frank said. "If orange is all around you in a pumpkin patch, what patch—of all the ones in Bayport—might you meet a wicked witch in?"

"The patch of the Wicked Witch of the West!" Callie said, her face lighting up. "Farmer West's pumpkin patch is out near the interstate!"

"That's a long, purposeless drive if we're wrong," Joe said. Then he smiled. "But I don't think we're wrong. Let's go!"

They ran back to the car, and quickly drove out to Farmer West's Country Restaurant and Farm. When the friends got there, the restaurant was bustling with activity. Cars and motorcycles lined the parking lot.

The farm had self-guided tours through a big corn maze stretching away from the restaurant and into West's fields. "The pumpkin patch is on the far side of the maze," Callie said.

They cut between the rows of dried corn—ignoring the paths of the maze—until they came to the broad swath of moonlit farmland beyond. As they emerged from the rustling stalks, they saw a huge orange, pyramidlike shape.

"That's got to be it," Joe said.

Sprinting forward, they discovered a twenty-foot-tall pyramid built out of pumpkins. Dried fields of corn came right up to the pyramid on three sides. Several big old logs had been set nearby as makeshift benches. Frank smiled and shook his head in admiration. "It must have taken someone a long time to build that pyramid," he said.

"The clue!" Callie called. "I found the clue!" She stooped down to pick up the fist-size, ceramic pumpkin. The brothers raced to her side.

As Callie held up her prize, the cornstalks rustled in the wind.

Suddenly, a rumbling filled the small clearing. All three teens looked up. The pumpkin pyramid was toppling toward them.

9 Sincerely Smashing Pumpkins

All at once a mountain of bright orange squash rained down on them. The brothers and Callie threw their hands over their heads for protection.

"Run!" Frank called. But it was too late.

The pumpkins pummeled the teenagers' bodies and tripped them up, sending them sprawling into the dry field. A cry came from the other side of the falling pyramid.

The rumbling avalanche seemed to last forever, though it couldn't have been more than a few seconds. When it subsided, a huge cloud of dust filled the air where the pyramid had been, and sticky orange pulp from shattered pumpkins covered the ground.

Frank Hardy slowly got to his feet and waved the

dust away from his face. "Joe! Callie! Are you all right?"

Several coughs came in reply—one from further across the jumble of orange carcasses. Spotting Callie's slender hand amid the pulpy rubble, Frank made his way to her side and helped her up. Almost simultaneously, Joe started to get up.

"I'm okay," Callie said. "Just got the wind knocked out of me."

"Me, too," Joe added. "And these pumpkins have seen better days."

A shadowy figure emerged from the other side of the pumpkin patch. "You guys owe me!" the shadow croaked.

Frank pulled his flashlight out and shone it on Brent Jackson. The football player looked battered and slightly soggy with orange pulp. "You did this to keep me from claiming the prize!" Jackson growled. "You owe me restitution!"

"What are you talking about?" Joe asked angrily. "We already got the prize."

"*Had* the prize, you mean," Callie said. "Sorry, guys. I lost it when the pyramid fell."

"It's got to be around here somewhere," Frank said, "even if it's buried under pumpkins." He began to look through the pumpkin wreckage.

"I saw it first," Jackson said. "You guys did this to keep me from getting it." He bent over and started rooting through the remains of the pyramid.

"Get lost, Jackson," Joe said. "We had that prize fair and square."

Jackson stood up. "Why don't we settle this here and now, Hardy."

"Why don't we," Joe replied. He tossed aside a piece of pumpkin shell and balled up his fists.

"This has to be the stupidest-looking thing I've ever seen," said a woman's voice.

All of them spun to see Missy Gates and Jay Stone, dressed in jeans and leather "Kings" jackets. They were standing at the edge of the cornfield.

"What are you doing here?" Jackson snapped.

"Looking for prizes," Missy replied. "Same as you. Find any, or are you just having a big pie fight?"

"We found one," Callie said, "but lost it when the pumpkin pyramid fell."

"I found it first!" Jackson said.

Missy laughed. "Is this what you're looking for?" she asked. She walked over between two rows of dried corn and picked up the broken pieces of a ceramic pumpkin.

"Is the prize envelope with it?" Frank asked.

Missy shook her head and tossed the pieces on the ground.

"Looks like someone beat you dopes to the punch," said Jay Stone.

"Maybe that someone was you!" Jackson snarled.

"He's right," Joe said. "Someone toppled those

87

pumpkins on us—and you two seem likely candidates."

"As if we're dumb enough to stick around after pulling something like that," Stone snorted.

"Someone who's smart might divert suspicion by sticking around and playing innocent," Frank said. "Though I suppose that smart part leaves you two out."

"Very funny, Hardy," Missy said. "It just so happens that I saw someone hightailing it out of here through the corn rows as we arrived."

"A likely story," said Callie.

Missy glanced around at the rubble before settling down on one of the logs at the clearing's edge. "Call the cops if you don't believe me," she said with a sly grin.

Stone stood beside her. "Don't mind us," he said. "We'll just watch while you swim in pumpkin slime."

Frank shook the pumpkin guts off his hands. "No sense doing that, if the prize has already been taken," he said.

"My guess," Missy said, "is that whoever knocked down the pyramid took the prize."

"That's possible," Joe said, wiping his hands on his coat.

"Well, I don't buy it," Jackson said. "I think one of you guys took my prize."

"Grow up, Jackson," Missy said. She stood up

and shoved an old log with the heel of her boot. The log rolled a half turn and bumped into the cornstalks. "C'mon, Jay," she said. "Let's leave these losers before losing rubs off on us." She turned and walked into the corn rows. Stone followed her.

"Nice that Missy's got a new dog," Joe said.

"Very funny, Hardy," Jackson said. "This isn't over, you know!" He gathered up the broken pieces of the ceramic pumpkin and stalked off into the corn.

"Now what do you suppose he wants with those pieces?" Callie asked.

"Maybe he's starting a collection," Joe suggested. "It's not like he's going to win anything."

Frank chuckled. "Missy Gates is clever," Frank said.

"What do you mean?" Joe and Callie asked simultaneously.

"She was trying to get everyone riled up, so we'd stop looking for clues," Frank replied. "But, if you remember, last time we solved a two-riddle puzzle it led to both a prize—which we didn't get—and a clue."

"On the roof of the antique store!" Callie said. "So there *must* be another clue around here somewhere."

Joe nodded. "And I think I know where." He walked to the log where Missy had been sitting and pulled it out of the cornstalks into its original position. The log made a vague clanking sound as he yanked on it. "This log is chained to some stakes," he said, "so no one can take it from the field. And check out the top."

Frank and Callie walked over and saw a message carved into the surface of the old wood: *To burn the runes he ran off track, but demon had him for a snack.*

"Clever girl," Callie said. "She thought by pushing the log over she'd hide the clue from anyone else who came to look."

"She didn't count on the Hardy brothers' keen powers of observation," Joe said, chuckling.

"Jackson was so riled up he missed it completely," Frank said.

"There was something about runes in a movie I saw once," Callie said. "I can't remember it right now, though."

"We're all tired," Frank said, "and it's after midnight anyway. We should go home and get some sleep. We'll think better in the morning."

They wrote the new clue below the two that had led them to Farmer West's pumpkin patch, and then went back to the van and headed home.

"Boy," Joe said after they dropped Callie off, "this case is something. We've got the mystery of the devil-masked man to deal with, the break-in at the vault, and the puzzles in the contest as well."

"It's hard to see how it might all fit together,"

Frank said. "Is there some conspiracy here, or just cutthroat competition?"

"We'll get a fresh start tomorrow," Joe said, yawning. "After school."

"I can't wait for Saturday," Frank said. "At least then we'll be able to sleep in before the contest starts up."

The high school buzzed with contest gossip the following morning. The *Bayport Chronicle* even ran a small story about the clues leading to the winning of the VW beetle; Allison proudly showed off the classic car before class.

"No doubt who's ahead in this competition," Joe said to Frank and Callie.

"Slow and steady wins the race," Frank reminded them.

"Then why do I feel like I've been run over?" Callie quipped.

Missy Gates took great delight in telling the tale of the pumpkin patch avalanche to anyone who would listen during the school day. At lunch people kept offering the Hardys and Brent Jackson pieces of pumpkin pie.

Callie put her lunch tray down on a table next to the Hardys. "I remembered the movie where I'd heard about runes," she said. "It was *The Rocky Horror Picture Show.* One of the songs says, 'Dana Andrews said prunes, gave him the runes.'"

Joe made a face. "What does *that* mean?"

"The music is very satirical," Callie said. "Maybe it's a reference to another film. *Rocky Horror* has lots of jibes at other movies."

"We can check it on the Internet," Frank said. "I'm sure there's a site or two devoted to *Rocky Horror* lyrics."

A web search during study hall turned up some information, but none of the three were feeling much further ahead at the end of the school day.

As darkness approached, the brothers picked up Callie and headed downtown for their first stop. As they neared the Book Bank, Callie spotted Missy Gates ahead of them. She was on a small motorcycle.

"Let's follow her," Callie suggested, "and see what she's up to."

"Okay," Frank said, checking his watch. "We've got a little time before the contest starts."

They followed Missy out to Magnum American Motors. She pulled into the small parking lot on the side of the building and walked toward the front door. The Hardys parked their van across the street, a short distance from the entrance. The corner of the building shielded them from Missy's view.

Missy stopped outside the door. They heard Howard "Harley" Bettis's voice.

"You can't come in," Bettis said. "The boss is out. He doesn't want my friends hanging around when he's out."

"When did you become such a stickler for rules?" Missy asked.

Harley grumbled. Missy laughed and walked through the door into the shop.

"Well, we already knew those two were in cahoots," Joe said.

Callie sighed. "We might as well get to the Book Bank and kick off tonight's treasure hunting." Frank turned the van around, and they drove to their usual parking spot by the river before hiking back to the Soesbees' bookstore.

They lined up with the other customers and picked up their three clues just after sunset. They chose Romero Remodeling as their second stop, and opened the clues as they walked there.

"Boy, I'm getting tired of duplicates," Joe said after examining the first one.

Frank shrugged. "There's a limited number of prizes, so there can only be a limited number of clues. I got us a free cup of coffee at Java John's, though." He held up the instant winner.

"Here's a new one," Callie said. *Sails may fray but these decay, where rigging webs the rafters.*"

"That sounds like boats," Joe said. "Didn't we have another clue about boats?"

"Yes!" Callie said, her eyes lighting up. "The one about Vanderdecken—he was the Flying Dutchman, a doomed mariner cursed to wander the seas." She fished into her purse and pulled out the old clue. *"Vanderdecken wouldn't be caught undead tying one on here."*

Frank gave her a quick hug. "You've been doing some research," he said. "Good work."

"'Tying one on' might not be a reference to beer," Joe said. "It could be about mooring boats."

"And where would rigging web the rafters and tied boats decay?" Frank said.

"At the old nautical warehouse!" they all said simultaneously.

"We were working on the floats near a clue and never even guessed!" Callie said.

"We can walk there from here," Frank said. "It's only a little farther than going back to the van."

"Let's hustle," Joe said, breaking into a jog.

They reached the old dock warehouse in under fifteen minutes. Sweating and out of breath, they opened one of the big, barnlike doors partway and slipped into the huge garage area where the floats were stored.

"The clue must be in one of the back rooms, or we'd have seen it while we were working on the floats," Callie said.

"Lead on," Frank replied.

Callie skirted around the Werewolf's Wagon and the other floats, and took them toward an unused storage area. They dodged around some big pieces of tackle and some other old fishing equipment, and they came to a worn door.

Frank pulled the door open, and they all walked into the large, junk-filled room beyond. A message had been hastily spray painted on one wall in large, red block letters: GRANTED DIRECTIONS, WITH ONE HITCH, TO ABANDON YOUR TRAILING.

Joe scratched his head. "Another mystery," he said.

"The prize!" Callie exclaimed, picking up a ceramic pumpkin. "This time, we're first, and no one can claim otherwise." She opened the pumpkin, took out the prize envelope, and smiled proudly.

Something rattled in the back of the room. Frank shone his flashlight in that direction.

A helmeted figure moved quickly through the shadows.

"Too late, pal," Joe said. "We got here first. You'll have to settle for the big clue."

As he said it, though, the figure pushed some fishing tackle at them and dashed out the door. The brothers had to dodge the debris and Callie tripped and fell back against the spray-painted wall.

Frank helped her up. "Are you okay?" he said. She nodded.

"I think we might have found our troublemaker," Joe said, running out after the helmeted man. Frank and Callie soon followed.

"You think there's a devil mask under that helmet?" Frank asked, following him.

"Let's catch him and find out," Joe replied.

95

The two of them burst into the float warehouse, with Callie close behind.

Suddenly, though, blinding headlights shone in their eyes, and a mighty engine roared.

The brothers spun around to see Dracula's Dragster bearing down on them full throttle.

10 Werewolf's Wagon vs. Dracula's Dragster

The big black float roared like a dragon as it sped across the concrete floor of the old dock warehouse. It was heading straight for Frank and Joe.

"Jump!" Frank said.

The brothers dove to either side as the float zoomed between them. Callie stepped out of the way to avoid being bowled over by Frank.

The dragster crashed through the half-open doors of the warehouse, flinging them wide as it skidded out onto the street.

Callie gave Frank a high five. "Thanks," he said. "Do you have the keys to that float you've been working on with Iola?"

Callie nodded and dug into her purse.

"C'mon, Joe," Frank called as Callie handed him the keys. "We're going after him."

The brothers sprinted to the girls' furry float and hopped in. Frank started the engine, and Joe moved a fake wolf's tail off of the windshield of the stripped-down pickup.

"Bring it back in one piece!" Callie shouted. Frank slipped the truck into gear and roared out of the warehouse.

"Call the cops!" Joe shouted back to her as they sped away.

The dragster didn't have a big head start, and both cars were old and hadn't been built for speed.

"Step on it, Frank!" Joe said.

"Pedal's already to the metal," Frank replied. "Let's just hope that dragster doesn't have any more horses than we do."

"Man," Joe said with a smile, "you think they'd put some more power in these floats!"

Both brothers laughed.

Dracula's Dragster wove through the streets. It was heading north from downtown. Werewolf's Wagon was close behind. Costumed prize-hunters pointed and stared as the floats zipped by.

The black car veered left on Howard, then right onto Phillips, passing the Dungeon Guild—the outermost shop participating in the Spooktacular.

They took a sharp right onto Ashton, heading east toward the river's bank. The rear end of the

Werewolf's Wagon skidded as Frank wheeled it around the corner. The tires howled and the back fender nearly smashed into a pile of trash cans stacked at the edge of the curb.

Frank fought for control, and soon brought the float back on course.

"He's headed for the park by the waterfront," Joe said, peering into the darkness after their enemy.

"Bad move," Frank replied. "There aren't a lot of roads down there, and they're all relatively straight. No way he can lose us in that park."

As they crossed Burlington Avenue, the black car suddenly veered off the road and cut diagonally through a small green, weaving around the benches and deserted playground equipment.

Frank took the long way around.

"Why didn't you follow?" Joe asked.

"This thing steers like a cow," the elder Hardy replied. "If I tried to take it through that park, we'd hit something for sure." He smiled grimly. "Besides, I'd rather not rip up public property if we don't have to. Don't worry, he won't gain much time with this trick."

By the time the Hardys rounded the park, Dracula's Dragster had opened up its lead by another half block—but they still had it well in sight.

"Now he's going for the beach area," Joe said as the black car veered right again.

"I see it," Frank said, cranking the wheel over.

The wagon squealed and shimmied as he guided it onto the curving road leading to Bayshore Drive.

The beach area officially closed at dusk, and the Spooktacular had drawn away the teenagers who usually hung out at the waterfront. The two cars tore down empty Bayshore Drive.

As they passed the beach, Dracula's Dragster took a sudden right turn into the beach parking lot.

"Now what's he up to?" Joe asked.

Frank swerved the Werewolf's Wagon into the lot as the dragster careened over the curb and onto the beach. The sedan's oversize tires kicked up huge clouds of dust as it skidded across the sand.

"Go for it, Frank!" Joe said.

Frank gunned the wagon's engine and zoomed onto the beach. He spun the wheel hard and angled after the stolen float. The wagon's motor whined as it worked hard to gain traction on the sand.

"We're losing him!" Joe said. "Keep up the speed!"

"I'm trying," Frank replied.

A small dune launched their front end into the air. The Werewolf's Wagon hit the sand hard. Its tires spun, digging into the powdery grit. With a sudden lurch, the car stopped, the tires still wailing, trying to gain traction in the sand.

Dracula's Dragster skidded off the beach and up the boat launch. Moments later, it zoomed back onto Bayshore Drive.

Frank shifted from forward to reverse and back again, hoping to extricate their vehicle from the sand. It was no use. He hit his palm on the steering wheel in frustration. "Those big tires really helped him out on the sand."

"We did what we could," Joe said. "He was lucky, that's all. I'll call the cops and tell them which way he's headed."

"Call Callie, too," Frank said. "Tell her to bring the van. We're going to need a tow off this beach."

An hour and a half later they'd towed the wagon back to the warehouse and cleaned it up. Officer Sullivan took their statements and informed them that Dracula's Dragster had been found a few blocks away from the beach.

"Near Magnum Motors," Joe whispered to Frank and Callie.

"Looks like it had been hot-wired," Sullivan said. "No sign of the culprit, though. You kids try and keep your noses clean from now on. I don't want to be seein' you again during this contest."

The Hardys and Callie got into the van and drove back to their parking spot by the river.

"We came so close!" Callie said, clearly frustrated. "We almost had him!"

"At least the bad guy didn't get the prize this time," Joe said. "By the way, what did we win?"

Callie slapped her forehead. "You know, I got so

wrapped up in this, I forgot to open the envelope! I'm surprised I remembered to write down the clue from the warehouse wall."

"Well?" Joe said. "Don't keep us in suspense."

They all gathered around while she fished the envelope out of her purse and tore it open.

"We've won two pairs of Walkabout walkie-talkies from Corman and Cross Electronics," Callie said with a smile.

"Cool," said Joe.

"Not a bad prize," Frank said. "They might even help with this investigation."

"Oh, so this is an 'investigation' now, not a contest?" said Callie.

"Well . . . it's *both*," Frank replied.

"We can swing up toward Corman and Cross and collect our prize as we gather more clues," Joe said.

"Who'll we give the fourth walkie-talkie to?" Callie asked.

"How about Iola," Joe suggested. "After the contest is over, of course. We wouldn't want anyone thinking she'd helped us win the prize."

Callie nodded. "Good deal. C'mon, let's get going. Thanks to that car chase, we're way behind on our clue collecting."

They walked down the park path toward Corman and Cross. Several costumed prize-hunters passed them, going the other way, heading over the footbridge into the heart of downtown.

"The guy that took Dracula's Dragster hot-wired it pretty quickly," Frank said.

"I noticed that, too," Joe replied. "Makes you think it might have been someone who works with cars."

"Or motorcycles," Frank said, nodding.

"Are you thinking Harley Bettis—or one of the other Kings?" Callie asked.

"Harley, mostly," Frank said. "As Joe noted, the stolen dragster ended up just a couple of blocks from Magnum American Motors."

"We could go ask Magnum where Harley's been tonight," Joe suggested. "Find out if he took a break around then."

"If you think he'd tell us," Callie said. "First things first, though. Let's pick up these walkie-talkies and grab some more clues. Otherwise, we'll be out of the hunt for good."

"Not completely," Joe said. "We know we got to that last clue before anyone else. That gives us a bit of an edge."

"Only if we can figure out what *Granted directions, with one hitch, to abandon your trailing* means," Callie replied. She pulled her letterman jacket tighter around her shoulders. "Are you guys cold, or is it just me?"

"Hang on a second," Frank said, coming to an abrupt stop. "Do you hear anything?" he whispered.

Joe and Callie stopped and listened.

"Voices?" Joe finally whispered. "So?"

"They're coming from those bushes," Frank replied. "There's no path through that stand of woods."

"So, they're not supposed to be there," Callie said. "And—if I heard right—they're talking about the contest."

Frank nodded. "I thought so, too."

"Well," Joe said, keeping his voice low, "let's sneak closer and see what we can hear."

Cautiously they moved off the path and toward the copse of spruce trees and evergreen bushes. As they drew close, the voices became clearer.

"If we work together, we can sew up a lot of these prizes," one muffled voice said.

"I'm for that," replied a second. "No sense letting the chumps cash in when we can do it ourselves."

"It's working so far," said a third. "I got a pretty good haul already." The voices were unrecognizable and sounded eerie in the autumn darkness.

The Hardys and Callie peered through bushes and saw three Halloween-masked figures huddled together in a tiny clearing. They all wore dark, bulky jackets and jeans.

"No devil mask in the bunch," Joe whispered.

"It's easy to change masks," Frank noted.

"So," the figure wearing a horribly scarred puppetlike fright mask said, "I've got an extra about burning monsters. Who wants it?"

"The *turn, turn* one?" said a conspirator in a Frankenstein's monster mask. "Already got it."

"Me, too," replied their wolf-faced companion. "And I've got the one that goes with it. Don't you have anything better to offer? I've got some prime goods here, but I'm not about to hand them over for that kind of garbage. I want to win big here, not pick up your trash."

Callie's brown eyes widened and she hissed to the brothers, "They're trading clues to fix the contest!"

11 The Unholy Three

Frank and Joe nodded. "Let's see how far they'll take it," Joe whispered.

The wolf-masked conspirator held up a clue. "I've got a sweet duplicate about a haunted car," the wolf's soft voice said. "I got the minor prize, but it leads to a big clue. What do you have to trade?"

"I've got one about some foreign guy," the monster replied. "I ain't figured it out yet."

"I'm looking for stuff about ships or UFOs," the one in the scar-faced fright mask said. "I've got mummies and cars to trade."

"The mummy clue has been solved," said the wolf. "This is getting us nowhere fast, and I want to get back in the game. Let's lay our duplicates out, and then see who wants to trade."

"Yeah, okay," the Frankenstein monster replied. He dug into his pocket and pulled out a handful of clues.

Scar Face nodded and did the same. "Hope you don't mind if I don't put 'em down," he said. "I don't entirely trust either of you."

"We don't trust you, either," the wolf said, holding out a half dozen clue cards. "Now, let's take a look, and see what we've got."

All three stared intently at each other's cards for a moment.

"An interesting way to play the game," Frank said, stepping through the trees and into the circle of conspirators. "Kind of like liar's poker."

"If any of you want to come clean about this," Joe added, following his brother, "I'm sure the *Bayport Chronicle* will be interested in hearing about your little alliance."

The three masked treasure hunters pocketed their clues, then turned and ran in opposite directions.

"I'll get Scar Face," Frank said, taking off after the one in the fright mask.

"Señor Stein is mine," Joe said, chasing the Frankenstein monster.

"Leave the wolf to me," Callie said, sprinting after the last of the group.

Scar Face sprinted away from the river, toward Perrin Avenue. Frank lit out after him, but the fright-masked conspirator was clearly in good shape. He hit the street first, then dodged into an alleyway.

Frank barreled across the street. Just then, a car turned the corner and bore down on him. The sedan's tires squealed and the driver leaned on the horn. The car pulled up short; unable to stop in time, Frank bounced lightly off the hood.

"Crazy kid!" yelled the driver.

"Sorry about that," Frank said, trying not to let his frustration show.

The car drove on. The elder Hardy sprinted to the alleyway, but found no sign of Scar Face.

The Frankenstein monster headed for the footbridge into downtown. Joe ran as fast as he could, but his muscles began to ache almost immediately. He and Frank had expended a lot of energy earlier, towing the Werewolf's Wagon out of the sand with their van.

Joe grimaced and tried for one last burst of speed. He caught up with the monster at the start of the bridge. The masked man, though, suddenly turned and rammed his shoulder into Joe's gut.

Caught off guard, the younger Hardy staggered back into the low railing of the bridge. He reeled there for a moment, on the verge of toppling over.

When he finally recovered, the monster was already disappearing into the shadows at the bridge's far end.

"Rats!" Joe said, kicking the bridge's wooden planking.

Frustrated, he turned and walked back to where he'd left the others. As he neared the small cluster of woods, he saw Frank returning from the opposite direction.

"Lost him," Joe said through gritted teeth.

"Me, too," Frank replied as they converged. "Where's Callie?"

"Right here," she called, coming down the path. "Good thing I'm a little more spry than you bruisers. Wolfie here almost made it to her bicycle, but not quite." She smiled and wheeled the bike over to the brothers. The wolf-masked conspirator followed close behind, snarling slightly.

"Allison Rosenberg, I presume—judging from the bike," remarked Joe.

"So what?" Allison said, pulling the wolf mask off her face. "There's no law against collaborating with other contestants. You three are doing it yourselves!"

"Why'd you run then?" Frank asked.

"I thought you were the masked bandit," she replied. "After the other night, I need to be careful."

"Which is why you were meeting two masked guys in the woods?" Joe said. "Sorry, Allison, I don't buy it."

"Okay," she said, "maybe I'm not proud of it— but trading clues has done me a lot of good. And I'm going to keep doing it; there's nothing in the rules to stop me."

"Who were those guys?" Frank asked. "Brent Jackson and Ren Takei, I'm guessing, judging by their size and the tone of their muffled voices."

Allison crossed her arms over her chest; her eyes narrowed. "Maybe I don't know who they are," she said.

"You're not that big a fool," Callie replied. "You wouldn't trust people you don't know—not after getting mugged the first night."

"Unless, of course," Joe said, "the mugging was part of some elaborate scheme to better your position in the game."

Allison's blue eyes burned with anger. "Give me back my bike," she hissed. "I haven't done anything wrong."

"Give it to her, Callie," Frank said. Callie handed over the bike. "We'll be keeping an eye on you, Allison. Someone is working hard to rig this contest—and you're one of the big winners so far," Frank stated.

Allison Rosenberg yanked her bike out of Callie's hand, mounted it, and rode away without another word.

"So much for that friendship," Joe said.

Frank shrugged. "We can apologize—if we need to—once we've figured all this out. C'mon. Let's go pick up those walkie-talkies before anything else happens."

They left the riverside park and went to Corman and Cross. Along the way, they saw a bunch of other contestants gathering clues. They didn't spot Allison, Ren, or Brent, though.

"I wouldn't be surprised if the three of them lay low for a while," Joe said, "to throw off suspicion, if nothing else."

They picked up their walkie-talkie prizes, then went to the pizzeria for a break.

"The two-mile range on these could come in handy," Frank said, fiddling with the two-way radios. He kept one for himself, gave two to Joe (one for Iola), and handed the last one to Callie. "I've put them all on the same frequency," he said. "I doubt we'll use them tonight, but just in case . . ."

Callie rifled through the six new clues they'd obtained, handing them to Joe as she finished. "Three duplicates—too bad we're not in Allison's trading group." She gave a weak smile. "A movie ticket instant winner, and a food prize for Kool Kone, which I guess we won't be using until this is over."

Joe shrugged. "Sorry," he said. "Jackson just ticked me off."

"What's the last one?" Frank asked.

"*A fishy destination fin-ished this space race,*" Callie said.

Joe ran his hand through his blond hair. "Doesn't sound like it fits with any of the others we've got," he said. "Though it might be part of that UFO puzzle that Scar Face was after."

Frank nodded. "Let's hit the C Cafe next. We can

go online there and research some of the things we already have."

"Good idea," Joe and Callie said.

The three of them finished their pizza and drinks, then headed out.

"If we cut through the alley behind the pizzeria," Joe said, "we can save some time." Frank and Callie nodded their agreement, and they cut around the back of the building.

The alley behind the pizzeria led down to the old Kwik-Fill on Kenosha Street. As they neared the gas station, they spotted Vincent Blasko talking animatedly on a public phone in the parking lot.

"Yes, I know how much I owe," Blasko said. "I didn't intend to run up those kind of debts—but these things happen."

"Hang on a minute," Joe whispered. He put his arm out and motioned Frank and Callie to stay in the shadows of the alleyway. They all stepped back against the wall of the building.

"I'll have the money soon," Blasko said. "Yes. *Very* soon. Perhaps as early as tomorrow if things work out."

He paused a moment. "Yes, I'm sure. No, I'm not having any trouble. Everything is working out just as planned. It's all fixed up. I told you, don't worry. This is a sure thing. The money is practically in my hands. Yes. I'll call when I have it. No, you can't call me. Good-bye."

Blasko slammed the receiver down and turned up Kenosha Street. He pulled a fruit pie from his pocket, unwrapped it, and began to munch as he walked away from the Kwik-Fill.

"That seems a little suspicious," Joe whispered.

"Do you think he was talking about fixing the contest?" Callie asked.

"I'm not sure," Frank replied, "but it seems like the best lead we've had so far. Someone who is on the inside, like Blasko, would have an easier time cheating."

"If he needs money, he might be willing to help some of the contestants to cash in—and then take a cut," Joe added.

"But who's his partner?" Callie said. "He can't enter the contest himself."

"Well, we know there are at least four people who will do most anything to win," Frank said.

"Allison Rosenberg, Ren Takei, Brent Jackson, and the Kings," Callie said.

"Right," Joe concluded. "Let's follow Blasko and see where he goes. He could be meeting someone. It means we won't collect any more clues tonight— it's too close to curfew—but I really want to get to the bottom of this."

"Me, too," Frank added.

Callie shrugged. "So much for the C Cafe."

"We can research on the Net tomorrow," Frank said. "Following Blasko won't wait."

The three of them stuck to the shadows as they followed the aging movie star. Blasko meandered down the sidewalks, keeping to the main roads until he reached the old Browning Theater.

It was now after midnight, and the theater was closed. Blasko looked in the front, and then walked around the alleyway to the back. The Hardys and Callie followed.

"What do you suppose he's doing here?" Joe whispered.

"Let's find out," Frank replied.

When they were halfway down the alley, they heard a door creak open. Moving quickly, Joe sprinted around the corner and caught it before it swung shut again. Peering into the darkness inside the back of the theater, they saw no sign of Blasko.

"He must have gone in, but I don't see him," Callie whispered.

"Me neither," Frank said.

"We should take a look inside," Joe said, "in case he's up to no good."

The others nodded, and they all moved cautiously into the darkened theater. "Keep your flashlights off," Frank cautioned. "We don't want him to know we're here."

They walked quietly from the rear exit to the stage area.

When it was first built, the Browning had been home to live performances. Later it was converted to a movie house. But though films now made up the vast majority of its business, the stage still retained all the accoutrements of a live theater.

Rigging ran high into the rafters, and catwalks arched above the stage. Ropes and pulleys operated the curtains, which were drawn back since the movie screen was lowered for the show earlier in the evening.

"I don't see anyone," Callie whispered. "It's quiet as a grave."

"I can hardly see *anything*," Joe complained. "Let's get out the flashlights."

Suddenly, a rope squealed—running fast through a pulley—as the theater's heavy fire curtain fell straight toward them.

12 Theater of Blood

The shiny gray curtain rained down on the startled teens.

"Everyone down!" Joe said, throwing himself flat on the floor. Frank and Callie did the same.

The heavy fabric landed on top of them with a loud "Whoomph!"

"Is everyone okay?" Frank called. He groped around, found Callie's hand, and squeezed it.

"I'm okay," she said. "How about you, Joe?"

"I feel winded," Joe said. "But it could be a lot worse. Find the edge. We have to get out from under this thing."

They all crawled around, searching for the curtain's edge. They found it near the front of the stage and pulled themselves out.

116

Joe dusted himself off. "We could really have been hurt by this," he said.

"Look out!" Callie cried.

Joe and Frank spun as Vincent Blasko charged toward them, a wooden plank clutched in his withered hands. Blasko raised the plank high. "Get out of here, you!" he screamed.

He swung the plank at them. Frank stepped back, and the edge of the wood whizzed past his chest.

"Vandals!" Blasko cried. His bloodshot eyes looked wild and unfocused, and his teeth were stained bright red—as though he had been drinking blood.

Callie jumped aside, barely avoiding the blow. "Mr. Blasko, stop!" she yelled.

Blasko tottered slightly as the heavy plank pulled him off balance.

Joe dove for him, throwing his arms around the aging horror star in a textbook tackle. Blasko fell backward and, as he did, Frank grabbed the piece of wood out of his hands.

"What's this all about?" Joe asked.

"Help! Police!" Blasko called.

Frank put his hand on Joe's shoulder. "Hold on, Joe," he said. He fished his flashlight out and turned it on so that the old man could see them.

"Mr. Blasko," Frank said, "it's Frank and Joe Hardy, and Callie Shaw. We met you at the kickoff party."

Blasko peered at them. "I'm sorry," he said. "I just

took my contacts out. I didn't recognize you. I thought you were burglars. What are you doing here?"

"We might ask you the same thing," Joe said, helping the movie star up.

Blasko dusted himself off. "The owner of this theater generously offered to let me use the spare room behind the projection booth for the duration of my stay in Bayport. I'm sorry if I scared you, but you scared me as well."

"B-but your *teeth* . . . !" Callie said.

"My teeth?" Blasko said. "What about them?"

"They're covered with blood," Joe replied.

"Take a look," Callie added, handing him a mirror from her purse.

Blasko opened the mirror and looked. Then he laughed. "It's the cherry fruit pies," he said. "I'm terribly fond of them, but they stain my dentures. I stepped out and bought a few at the Kwik-Fill just a little while ago."

"Why would a big star like you be staying in an old theater like this?" Frank asked. "I know they're showing a festival of your films, but . . . Surely you can afford better."

Blasko looked around somewhat nervously. "I cannot. My finances have fallen on difficult times since the erroneous reports of my death. I cashed in my apartment downtown to save money."

"Then that's why you were on the phone talking about owing money," Callie blurted.

"You were listening?" Blasko said, shocked.

"We've been wondering about you since the other night at the Book Bank," Frank said. "Just after you left, we found out that someone had broken into the store."

"And whoever it was locked us in the vault," Joe said.

"Oh dear," Blasko replied. "I'm sorry to hear that. There's a simple explanation for why I was there, though. I had hoped that Ms. Soesbee might advance me the rest of my appearance fee, so that I could pay off some of my bills. Sadly, the store was closed. Honestly, I know nothing about any vault or break-in. Now, what are you doing here?"

"After we accidentally overheard you on the phone," Frank said, "we decided we should follow you. Someone's been messing with the Spooktacular, and, after what we heard, we thought it might be you."

"We think that someone is trying to rig the contests," Joe said.

"We're trying to put a stop to it," Callie added.

"Well, I must say that I admire your determination," Blasko said. "Though when I thought you were burglars you nearly scared the fangs out of me!" He put his withered hand over his heart. "Now I know how Christopher Lee felt every time Peter Cushing popped up in those old Dracula movies."

Frank snapped his fingers. "Cushing was Van Helsing, wasn't he?"

"That's right," Blasko said. "And Lee was Dracula."

The elder Hardy turned to Joe and Callie. "In that clue we have, what if *Vlad* and *Van* aren't references to the characters, but to the actors who played them?"

"That's it, Frank!" Callie said.

"We could do an Internet search and see what we turn up," Joe added.

"Well," Blasko said, showing his red teeth again, "if I've helped you in some way, I'm happy to have done so. Sorry about the curtain—and terribly sorry about the plank. Now, if you'll excuse me, I need some rest. Tomorrow is the big finish, you know."

"Thanks, Mr. Blasko," Joe said. "Sorry we scared you. We'll hoist the fire curtain before we go."

"I would be much obliged if you did," Blasko said.

While Blasko put away the piece of wood, the three friends used the pulley system to haul the heavy curtain back into the rafters. Finally, they bade Blasko good night and walked back to the van.

"Do you buy his story?" Joe asked.

"It makes sense," Frank said, "but he could still be part of the trouble. Money is a powerful motive. We'll have to stay on our toes."

"I think he's just a nice old man," Callie said.

"Who happens to make a living playing vampires," Joe added.

Callie shrugged. "Playing the undead beats *being* one."

"Have you guys been listening to the local news?" Callie asked as she walked into the Hardys' kitchen late the next morning. Joe and Frank sat at the breakfast table, looking worn out from all their treasure hunting.

Frank shook his head. "We just got up a little while ago," he said.

"Our brains aren't working yet," Joe added. "Want some eggs, or an English muffin?"

"A muffin, thanks," Callie said, taking a seat beside them. "There was a report on WBPT called 'Local Teens Capture Contest.' They interviewed Allison, because she's won so many prizes. She picked up a leather jacket last night."

"She's been on a roll," Joe said. "No doubt about it."

"With a little help from her friends," Frank added.

"They also talked about Ren Takei," Callie continued. "In addition to the handheld computer, he's won a pager, a skateboard, and Bayport Barons tickets. Even Brent Jackson has won some books from the Book Bank and a free oil change."

"At least the oil change will do him some good," Joe said. "I don't think he's cracked a book in his life."

"Allison hinted that she's closing in on some major prizes," Callie said. "She seemed very sure of herself."

"She should be," Frank replied. "She's clearly done better than the rest of the kids in school—including us."

"We'd be doing better if we weren't wrapped up in this mystery," Callie said. "And today's the last day of the contest."

"We may pull out a big win yet," Joe said.

"Anyway," Callie said, pushing back her chair, "I thought you'd want to know." She finished her muffin and headed toward the door. "I've got to help Iola with the float. The parade's tonight, you know, just before the contest ends."

"We'll drop by and pick you up later," Frank said. "Joe and I need to do some research first."

"And some brainstorming," Joe added. "Maybe now that we've a good night's rest we can figure out what's going on in this case."

The brothers worked on their computers and exchanged ideas all day long. But when it came time to pick up Callie at the old dock warehouse, they still hadn't found anything.

"There must be clues we're missing," Frank said to Callie, "both in the contest and in the case."

"Then we'll just keep at it," Callie said, "until we can make all the puzzle pieces fit."

"At least we turned up some things in our research," Joe said. He turned the van onto Racine Street, and headed for the Book Bank.

"Like what?" Callie asked.

"I checked on the actor Dana Andrews," Frank replied. "Though he was mentioned in the opening, he wasn't actually in *Rocky Horror*—but he *was* in a movie called *Curse of the Demon*. I found a summary on the Web. In the film, an evil magician tries to summon a demon to kill the Andrews character. But Andrews turns the tables, and the demon kills the sorcerer instead. The final scene of the movie takes place in a train yard."

Callie's eyes lit up. "That explains the '*ran off track*' part of *To burn the runes he ran off track, but demon had him for a snack*. It's a train reference."

"I thought so, too," Frank said. "Though I'm not sure how it ties into the contest."

"Hang on," Joe said. "I just remembered something. When I was checking on Cushing and Lee, I found a lot of Dracula movies—but I also found one called *Horror Express*. Remember the clue *Vlad and Van took the trip, but not in their usual seats*? That could mean both actors were in the picture, but not as Vlad and Van Helsing."

"And *trip* and *seats* could be a reference to traveling by rail," Callie added.

"So we have two train references," Frank said. "But where do they lead us? There aren't any famous train museums or shops in Bayport."

Joe nodded. "And there are too many local train tracks and terminals to just check them all, hoping to find a prize or another clue."

Callie sighed. "Maybe there's another clue in the series that we're missing."

"Let's pick up our clues at the Book Bank," Frank said. "With luck, that will give us something more to work with."

They stopped in at the bookstore. Kathryn and Daphne were working extra hard. Chet bustled around, helping them out. Iola had stayed at the old warehouse to put the final touches on the float before the parade.

The brothers and Callie lined up at the register and, when darkness fell, they picked up their clues for the night. The three of them went outside and checked their envelopes.

"Another Kool Kone certificate," Joe said, "to file for later." He smiled and stuffed the prize into his pocket.

"No wood in this undead camp, just the brainy taste of Naugahyde," Callie read. "Ick!"

"That's as cryptic as the rest," Joe said.

"Try this, then," Frank replied. *"Riding chopper failed to get ahead stalking Carl; Would a handgun have helped?"*

"Hey," Joe said. "I think I know that one. There used to be a show called *Kolchak: The Night Stalker.*

The main character was a reporter named Carl. He once got chased by a headless motorcyclist."

"Was he caught?" Callie asked.

"Nope," Joe replied. "They failed to get *a head*."

Frank laughed at his brother's joke. "That explains the first part of the riddle," he said. "And the second might be a location clue."

"*Handgun* could be Magnum—of Magnum American Motors," Callie said.

Frank nodded. "That's what I was thinking."

"Let's go," Joe said. The three of them jogged off toward the cycle shop.

The chime on the door rang as they let themselves in, but no one came to greet them.

"That's funny," Callie said. "I wonder where Harley and Mr. Magnum are."

"I think I've found one of them," Joe said.

He pointed to the floor where a pair of black boots protruded from behind the sales counter.

13 Parade of Death

Rod Magnum lay prone on the floor behind the long, Formica-topped desk. An antitheft monitor installed under the countertop cast pale light on his still form.

"Is he dead?" Callie asked as they raced to Magnum's side.

The shop owner groaned as Frank knelt down beside him.

"Just knocked out," the elder Hardy replied.

"I'm okay," Magnum said groggily. "Who hit me?"

"We don't know," Joe said. "We just got here." He gave Magnum a hand and the store owner slowly climbed to his feet.

Magnum rubbed his head.

"You should see a doctor," Callie said. "Blows to the head can be serious."

"No," Magnum replied. "I'll be okay. Motorcycle riders are used to getting banged around." He leaned heavily on the counter and tried to regain his bearings.

"Was it a robbery?" Joe said. "Is anything missing?"

Magnum looked around, and his eyes grew wide. "My clues!" he said. "The contest clues I had for tonight are gone!"

Frank's keen eyes caught a flash of movement on the monitor under the desk. A hooded figure skulked near the shop's rear door.

"There's someone out back," Frank said. "Joe, go out front. Maybe we can catch him."

"I'll stay here and help Mr. Magnum," Callie called after them.

Frank raced toward the back door as Joe burst through the front. The elder Hardy hit the door at almost full speed, but the lurker must have heard him coming. As Frank exited the rear of the shop, the shadowy figure was already running down the alley.

Frank nearly tripped over a smoking trash barrel that the intruder had left in his way. He brushed past it, sending cinders dancing into the windy autumn darkness.

By the time Frank hit the street, the running figure—dressed in jeans and a hooded gray sweat-shirt—was already a block ahead.

"Did you catch him?" Joe asked, circling around from the front.

"No," Frank called. "He's headed for the parade route!"

Both brothers sprinted after the suspect. As they neared Racine Street, they started to run into crowds. Onlookers lining up for the parade hindered the culprit—as well as the Hardys.

Cutting between groups of people, Joe caught up with his older brother. "I have a hunch about who we're chasing," Joe said.

Frank nodded. "Me, too. The only way to know for sure who it is, though, is by catching him."

The parade route ran along Main Street, which was parallel to Racine. As the brothers neared Main, the sounds of the parade drifted through the cool air. The crowds thickened, and soon the Hardys found themselves winding through the throng, only a few dozen steps behind the suspect.

The disguised person glanced back, but shadows hid his face. As soon as he saw the brothers closing on him, he darted out of the crowd and into the street—just as Dracula's Dragster rumbled past.

With many hurried apologies, Joe and Frank pushed their way through the crowd, and onto the street.

The hooded man ran around the dragster, and headed for the crowd on the far side of the street. As he did, Officer Sullivan stepped out and blew his whistle. "Hey you!" he said. "You're not part of the parade!"

The culprit turned and ran up the street, into a bevy of youngsters dressed as dancing pumpkins.

"You take one side, I'll take the other," Frank called to Joe. "We'll trap him between us."

The brothers fanned out to either side of the dance troupe, trailing just behind the hooded man. Before they could catch him, though, he broke through the front of the group and dashed into the marching band. He darted left, toward Frank. Just before Frank could grab him, he threw a shoulder block into a nearby drummer. The drummer tripped and crashed into Frank.

As Frank disentangled himself from the drummer, the hooded man tried for the sidelines again. But another policeman ran forward, joining Officer Sullivan in the chase.

The hooded man darted left again, with Joe hot on his heels. He climbed on the back of an elaborate Halloween float that was decorated as a haunted forest.

Joe vaulted up onto the float. The hooded man spun, aiming a kick at Joe's head. Joe ducked back, nearly falling off the moving vehicle. The fugitive darted between the papier-mâché and chicken-wire trees, and headed for the front of the float.

The younger Hardy scrambled to his feet just as Frank caught up with the float. Joe ducked around a fake tree and leaped forward, grabbing the hooded man with a shoestring tackle.

The man fell forward, crashing hard into one of the trees. The culprit grunted. Before he could get up, both Joe and Frank were on him.

The Hardys grabbed the suspect by either arm and held him down while Officer Sullivan and the other police arrived. Under the hood, the culprit was wearing a Frankenstein mask. "We've met before, I think," Frank said.

The monster struggled in the brothers' grip. Joe pulled the mask off. "Just as we thought," the younger Hardy said, "Brent Jackson."

"Why'd you run from Magnum Motors, Brent?" Frank asked.

"I looked through the window," Jackson said, "and saw Magnum on the floor. I thought you guys had put him there. I decided I better get the cops."

"You've got them, all right," Joe said. He and Frank hauled Jackson to his feet and turned him over to Sullivan and the other police who were converging on the float.

"What's going on here?" Sullivan asked.

"Someone knocked out Rod Magnum in his store," Joe said, "and we found this guy fleeing the scene."

"They're lying," Jackson said. "They're the ones who clubbed Magnum."

"Which is why he ran over the marching band,"

Frank said sarcastically. "He's got nothing to hide."

"I haven't heard anything about any trouble at Magnum's," Sullivan said, "but I'm inclined to bring all of you in."

"We were just trying to stop this guy," Joe explained. "He's the one who caused all the trouble."

"The kid's right, Gus," said a policewoman who had arrived just after Officer Sullivan. "It was Frankenstein here who was causing all the trouble." The parade had halted around them.

"You can't take me in and not take them, too," Jackson protested.

"Just watch me, smart guy," Sullivan said. He and the other officers took Jackson off the float. "And you Hardy boys," Sullivan added, "don't go anywhere we can't find you. Chief Collig may want to talk to you."

"Officer Con Riley has our number if you need us," Frank replied. He and Joe got off the float and headed back the way they'd come. They were now closer to the van than to Magnum Motors, so they picked up the car and headed back to the motorcycle shop.

The trouble along the parade route had turned the whole downtown area into a clog of bewildered people. The parade was having trouble restarting, and tempers had begun to flare. The police had their hands full trying to keep the disappointed crowds under control.

"Man," Joe said, "Jackson really started something ugly."

"I'm sure it'll calm down soon enough," Frank replied. He guided the van through the back streets and around the end of the parade route, and finally back to a parking space in front of Magnum American Motors.

"That's funny," Joe said as he opened the front door. "I'd have thought the cops would still be here."

"How's Magnum?" Frank asked Callie.

"Okay," Callie said. "He wouldn't let me call the police, though."

"I don't want any trouble," Magnum said.

"Well," Joe replied, "you've got trouble, whether you want it or not. Brent Jackson disrupted the parade and stirred up the whole town. He's the one we saw running from the back of the shop."

"It wasn't Harley Bettis?" Callie asked. "I was sure it would be him or one of the other Kings."

"Why would Bettis slug me?" Magnum asked.

"He and his friends tend to play by their own rules," Frank said. "Where is he, by the way?"

"He took the night off," Magnum replied.

"Have you seen any of Bettis's friends lurking around?" Joe asked. "Do you think they could be involved in this with Jackson?"

"I told you," Magnum said, "I didn't see anyone. You guys were the first to come into the shop since the contest started tonight—not counting whoever hit me."

"What about your video surveillance," Joe asked, looking at the monitor beneath the counter. The black-and-white screen showed views outside the front and back doors, as well as several points within the shop. "It must have caught Jackson—or whoever hit you—on tape."

Magnum shook his head, clearly puzzled. "I forgot to put a new cassette in earlier. The old one ran out, and then I got distracted with a customer."

Frank and Joe exchanged frustrated glances.

"You still need to call the police, Mr. Magnum," Callie said. "They'll want to know about the theft."

"They may already be on their way here," Frank added. "We mentioned the theft when we caught Jackson."

"I'll talk to the cops," Magnum replied. "I'm just glad you kids came in when you did. Why *did* you come in by the way? I'm afraid I'm out of clues."

"Actually, we came because of a clue," Joe said. "*Riding choppers failed to get ahead stalking Carl; Would a handgun have helped?* So, can you help?"

Magnum laughed.

"I was wondering when someone would figure out one of my prizes," he said. Walking to one of the parts shelves, he took down a box with a new motorcycle helmet in it. "Show me the clue and it's yours," he said.

133

Joe pulled out the paper and Magnum gave him the box. "Congratulations," the store owner said, making a note in his contest journal. "It's a top of the line model. Maybe I should have been wearing it myself." He rubbed the back of his head gingerly.

"You haven't had anyone claim the Geronimo then?" Frank asked.

Magnum shook his head. "Too bad," he said. "I could use the publicity."

"Mr. Magnum," Frank said, "do you think the thief could have burned the clues after taking them? I nearly ran into a smoking trash can while I was chasing Jackson; it looked as though someone had been burning papers in it."

"Oh, that was me," Magnum said. "I was getting rid of some old sales documents earlier. You weren't hurt, were you?"

Frank shook his head. "We should get going," he said.

"Good luck with the rest of the contest," Magnum replied.

"Don't forget to talk to the police," Callie added as they left.

"I'm calling them right now."

The clamor of bustling crows nearby drifted to the brothers and Callie as they climbed into the van.

"What do you think is going on?" Callie asked.

"I'm not sure, but let's figure it out," Joe said. He

drove the van down the street. They found some stragglers from the rest of the parade throng.

Frank leaned out the van window and asked, "What's going on?"

"Some of the contest officials are up in arms," replied a parade-goer dressed in a Star Trek uniform. "I heard they're marching up Racine Street to confront one of the organizers—the lady who wrote the riddles."

"Oh, no!" Callie said. "That means they're headed for the Book Bank!"

14 Witch Hunt

"Chill out," Joe said. "We can still get there before the mob does."

From where they were, they had a good view down Main Street. A police escort was keeping things orderly, but the people in the large group of parade-watchers—many of them in costume—looked like a mob out of a horror flick.

Joe skirted around the remains of the parade route, then cut down Racine Street toward the Book Bank. When they pulled up in front, they found the place dark and a "Closed" sign hanging in the window.

Callie frowned.

"You don't think Chet's gone out for food again, do you?" she asked.

Frank walked up the short flight of steps and rapped on the door. "Ms. Soesbee? Daphne? Chet? Open up! It's Frank, Joe, and Callie."

The curtain covering the window in the door cracked open, and someone fiddled with the lock from the inside. The door swung open, and the three teenagers entered.

"I'm glad you're here," Kathryn Soesbee said nervously. "One of my friends uptown called, and said there was a mob headed this way. Some of the other organizers are with them. There's been some kind of trouble with the contest, and I think they blame me."

"But you didn't have anything to do with Jackson messing up the parade," Joe said.

Chet and Daphne emerged from the back of the store. "I heard on the radio that there's been trouble with some of the clues," Chet said, "like what happened at Farmer West's the other night."

"That's not Ms. Soesbee's fault, either," Frank said.

"It sounds like people are getting *really* into this contest," Daphne said.

"If this blows up on us," Ms. Soesbee said, "it could ruin the store. We've had enough trouble keeping our heads above water since the big chain bookstore opened at the mall."

"Well, you can't solve this problem by locking the doors and turning out the lights," Frank said.

Kathryn Soesbee sighed. "You're right, of course," she said. "Turn on the lights, Daphne. I'll open the doors."

A wave of angry noise indicated that the mob was coming up Racine Street. Ms. Soesbee, Frank, Joe, and Callie went out on the front steps to meet it—leaving Daphne and Chet to mind the store.

The people in the crowd looked ugly, and not just because many of them were wearing Halloween costumes. At the front was Mr. Scott, and several other members of the Chamber of Commerce. Most of the rest seemed to be just people who joined the crowd along the parade route. They all made angry noises as they approached the bookstore. The few police who came along didn't look really equipped to enforce security.

"This has gotten entirely out of hand, Ms. Soesbee," Mr. Scott said. "Teenagers are running rampant in the street because of this silly contest." He looked a little ridiculous in his overstuffed scarecrow costume, but his voice was dead serious.

"You didn't think it was silly when you and the rest of the chamber agreed to it," Kathryn Soesbee said, putting on her bravest face.

"That was before we started to hear about trouble with the clues," Scott said.

"What trouble?" Ms. Soesbee replied. "Distribution of the clues has been scrupulously fair. Everyone has had plenty to give away."

"But some of the clue areas have been dangerous. The old warehouse, for example."

"Kids were working on parade floats there," Callie said. "How dangerous could it be?"

"What about reports of criminal activity, then?" Scott asked. "Clue stealing, someone taking a float for a joy ride, and the incident with the parade tonight?"

"You can't blame everyone for a couple of bad apples like Brent Jackson," Joe said.

The crowd grumbled angrily, clearly not pleased with the answers they were getting.

"The police are agitated as well," Mr. Scott added. "I've half a mind to call this whole thing off."

"But you *can't*," Callie said. "Think of all the people who are having fun."

"I don't think the disturbance tonight is much fun," Scott replied. "Some people are saying that this is all a plot to stir up publicity for the Book Bank."

"That's absurd," Ms. Soesbee shot back. "How could this kind of thing help my bookstore's sales? I'll be lucky if it doesn't ruin me! We can't cancel the contest at this late date. Every merchant downtown has too much invested in it."

"The woman is right!" said a deep voice from the back of the crowd.

Everyone turned to see Vincent Blasko pushing his way to the front of the mob. He was dressed in an elegant black suit and vampire cape.

Blasko mounted the steps. "Think of all those who have invested their time and effort in this contest. Not just the merchants, but the good people playing the game. They have devoted five days of their lives to solving these riddles—seeking these treasures. It would be a crime not to let them continue—despite the trouble.

"Troubles, after all, can be worked out." He smiled, showing his pointed teeth. "I myself am living proof of that. They declared me dead, but here I am." He turned in a circle so that everyone in the crowd could see that he was very much alive. "Here we all are, working together to solve the clue mysteries, to win the prizes—and to bring a little bit of fun and pageantry to Bayport. I say, the show must go on! What do you say?"

Blasko held his hand to his ear and the crowd bellowed, "The show must go on!"

Jay Stone and Missy Gates, in the back of the crowd, thrust their fists into the air and yelled, "Yeah!"

"Now," Blasko said, "I suggest that we leave these talented people and law-enforcement officials to sort things out. They are more than capable of doing so. As to the rest of us . . . the game is still alive!" With a quick nod to Kathryn Soesbee, Blasko led the mob back toward the center of town. Only a few cops, Mr. Scott, another member of the

Chamber of Commerce, and a reporter lingered behind.

The reporter stepped forward. "Ms. Soesbee," he asked, "do you think that the recent troubles have poisoned the results of the contest?"

"Not for me," she replied. "I've done my best to make the contest fair."

"The chamber will make sure that all results are impartial," Mr. Scott added.

"Why don't you follow Vincent Blasko," Joe suggested. "He seems to be the real story tonight."

The reporter looked from the small crowd in front of the bookstore to the throng moving back toward downtown. He shrugged and followed Blasko and the rest of the crowd.

Kathryn Soesbee let out a long sigh of relief.

"I'm still concerned about the disbursement of the prizes, Kathryn," Mr. Scott said after all the rest had gone. "A lot of the big awards haven't been collected yet—and a few people have won quite a large percentage of the prizes."

"The contest rewards hard work and creative thinking. Some people are obviously better at it than others," Ms. Soesbee replied. "No matter what, we *will* award the grand prize. The rest is up to the individual sponsors. That's what we all agreed on."

Mr. Scott loosened the collar of his scarecrow suit. "But there's very little time until midnight."

Ms. Soesbee shrugged. "Maybe that will make everyone more anxious to try again next year—*if* we do it next year. Why don't you come in and we can discuss this. My daughter has put on a fresh pot of coffee—and I have to get back to tending the store."

Mr. Scott, the other chamber member, and one of the policemen decided to stay; the other cop went back to his beat.

The Hardys and Callie stayed outside and breathed a sigh of relief.

"I'd say Mr. Blasko earned his pay tonight," Callie said.

Frank and Joe nodded.

Suddenly Frank said, "Callie, what's that splotch of red on your jacket?"

"What splotch?" she asked.

"I didn't notice it before, either," Joe said. "But it's really obvious in this light."

Frank loaned Callie his coat as she took her letterman jacket off. They all examined it—first, under the light of the streetlight nearby, and then with their flashlights.

"It looks like paint," Frank said. "It's almost invisible against the crimson of the fabric under normal light, but the orange streetlight makes it look black."

Callie ran her fingers over the stain. "It's dry at least," she said. "But I can't imagine where it came from. I washed it just a couple of days ago. The stain wasn't there then."

"Hey, wait a minute," Joe said. "See these long lines? They look like parts of a letter."

"Callie," Frank said, "didn't you bang your back against the wall in the warehouse the other day— just before the helmeted guy hijacked Dracula's Dragster?"

"You're right," she said. "The stain must have come from the clue on the wall. It was painted in dripping red letters."

"But Ms. Soesbee would have had to set up that clue days before," Joe said. "The paint couldn't have still been wet."

Frank nodded slowly, and his lips pulled into a grim smile. "The *original* paint couldn't have been wet," he said. "Come on. We're going to check that clue again."

Hopping in the van, it only took them a few minutes to get back to the abandoned room in the old warehouse.

"You're right, Frank," Joe said, as they carefully examined the lettering on the wall. "Someone has altered this message. The colors of paint are just slightly different."

"That's why the lettering on the last word looks so cramped," Frank said. "When we first saw it, I thought it was just quickly written. Callie must have bumped against the wet paint when she hit the wall."

"Here's what they used to rewrite it," Callie said,

holding up a spraycan of red paint. "The guy in the helmet must have dropped this when we spotted him."

"Which is why he ran," Joe said. "We knew he was up to no good—now we know *what* he was up to."

"So the real clue reads, *Granted directions, with one hitch, to abandon your rail*," Callie said.

"That makes much more sense," Frank said.

"It does?" Callie replied.

"It does if you're a suspense movie fan," Joe said. "Replacing *'rail'* with *'trailing'* threw the whole thing off."

"Cary Grant starred in a Hitchcock movie in which he rode on a train," Frank said.

"And the title of the movie is a direction," Joe added. *"North by Northwest."*

"That's the *rail* connection!" Callie said. "It fits in with the Vlad and the Demon clues."

"And gives us the direction we need for the other two train clues we already have," Frank said, smiling.

"There's an old abandoned *Northwestern* railroad trestle north of town," Joe said. "That must be where we need to go."

"Okay, I get that," Callie replied. "But why would anyone try to sabotage a clue?"

"Maybe so they could claim the prize for themselves," Frank said. "Though there's another reason I can think of, too."

144

"We'll find out for sure when we get there," Joe said.

It was just after eleven thirty when the three teens parked their van near the old train tracks. They scrambled down the overgrown slopes toward the old railroad bridge.

As they approached the bridge, a figure emerged from the bushes nearby.

"The devil-masked man!" Callie whispered.

15 Horror Express

"I think I see the clue against a girder near the center of the trestle," Joe said, peering into the darkness.

"Looks like Devil Mask spotted it, too," Frank said.

He, Joe, Callie, and the masked person sprinted toward the decaying bridge at the same time.

The Hardys reached the bridge just a second ahead of their rival. The devil-masked man scooped up a long, straight tree branch. He ran toward the Hardys.

Joe and Frank turned to protect themselves as the masked man bore in on them, swinging the branch.

"This is the last prize you'll try to steal," Frank said. He ducked under the branch and aimed a karate chop at the man's neck.

The devil-masked man stepped back, but the nostrils of the mask's long nose got stuck on Frank's fingers. With a rubbery ripping sound, the mask tore from their opponent's face.

"Ren Takei!" Callie gasped.

"With Jackson in the slammer, it was either him or Bettis," Joe said. "Frankly, I'm a bit surprised it wasn't Harley and his buddies."

"Using the devil mask for your crimes and the scar-faced mask for your more friendly meetings," Frank said. "Pretty clever idea."

"It kept you guessing," Takei said. "You'll never prove any of this, you know." Joe threw a punch at him, but he stepped nimbly back out of the way and counterattacked with his branch.

Joe ducked and backed away. The three young men stood equally spaced, in a momentary face-off.

"Give up," Frank said. "You can't take both Joe and me."

"Tell you what," Takei said. "We'll split this prize three ways. If I hadn't overheard you in the warehouse just now, I might never have figured out that clue anyway—so it's only fair."

"What do you mean?" Joe said. "You're the one that altered that clue."

Ren Takei shook his head. "Not me. I only got that clue tonight—just before I overheard you."

At that moment a light flared on the other side of the tracks, and a powerful engine roared.

"Of course!" Joe said, his blue eyes flashing with sudden insight.

"Is that Bettis?" Callie asked.

"Never mind, Callie," Frank shouted. "Call the cops!"

"I left my phone in the van!" she cried.

"Run back and call then!"

"We'll cover your back," Joe added.

She turned and sprinted toward the parked van.

With a sound like thunder, the big black motorcycle zoomed over the bridge toward the Hardys and Takei.

"Are you working with this guy?" Joe asked Takei.

A smile crept over Ren Takei's face. "I am now," he said, swinging the staff at Frank's head.

Frank dove to the side, barely avoiding being hit. Joe tried to help, but Takei twirled the stick around and stabbed it at him.

The motorcycle roared into the group, its black-helmeted rider swinging a chain. Frank and Joe ducked, and the chain passed over their heads. Takei, though, had to fend it off with his stick. The chain wrapped around the makeshift staff and ripped the weapon from Takei's hand. The branch sailed through the air and clattered onto the boards of the decaying trestle, several yards away.

"Hey! I'm on your side!" Takei cried, diving out of the cyclist's way at the last moment.

The black rider turned around and came back

for another pass, spinning the chain over his head once more. Takei tried to scramble out of the way again, but his foot got caught between two of the bridge's rotting boards. He ducked, but the chain grazed his temple. He fell onto the bridge, unconscious.

"Joe, go for the prize pumpkin," Frank called. "It must be what this guy wants!"

"Got it!" Joe said, racing toward the orange ceramic jack-o'-lantern.

The cyclist turned directly toward Joe and rocketed forward. He took a halfhearted swing at Frank as he passed, but the older Hardy easily ducked under the chain.

As the rider passed by, Frank scooped up Takei's lost staff and swung it hard into the cyclist's lower spine. The rider jerked backward and his motorcycle shot out from under him.

The bike smashed into the side of the bridge and stopped abruptly. The cyclist groaned and got to his knees. Frank charged at him, but the helmeted man threw his chain at the elder Hardy.

The chain caught Frank full in the chest. The air rushed out of his lungs and he staggered back. The leather-clad cyclist rose to his feet.

As he did, though, Joe hurtled into his knees from behind. The man collapsed like a sack of flour, right into Frank's waiting fist.

Frank hit him just below the ribs. The rider let

out a surprised gasp and fell to the ground. His helmeted head bounced against the old railroad tracks and he lay still.

The brothers stood above their defeated foe as blue police lights flashed over the nearby hills. The sounds of sirens filled the chilly autumn air.

Frank reached down and pulled the helmet from the black rider's head.

"Rod Magnum," he said.

"Which would make the prize in this pumpkin the limited edition Geronimo motorcycle . . ." Joe said. He tossed the small orange sphere casually into the air and caught it again. ". . . And the cause of all this trouble."

"There were two tricky parts of this mystery," Frank said as he sipped coffee the next morning. The brothers, Callie, the Mortons, and the Soesbees had gathered together at the Book Bank to celebrate the end of the contest. They all sat on chairs around one of the store's reading tables, sharing coffee and donuts.

"First was that there were *two* main culprits," Joe continued. "Ren Takei, and Rod Magnum."

"They weren't working together?" Iola asked.

"No," Callie said, "which was confusing. Takei was just out for prizes—any way he could get them. He didn't know anything about Magnum."

"So Ren was the devil-masked man," Daphne said.

"And he was also the man in the scar-faced mask who was trading clues with Allison," Joe added.

"Which is pretty ironic," Chet said, "considering he stole clues from her the first day."

"He was playing all sides of the game," Frank said, "both legal and illegal. He nearly clobbered us at Pratt's windmill, and then again at the West's pumpkin farm."

"And both times he got away with the prizes," Joe concluded. "He wasn't so lucky when he tried the same stunt last night."

"I can't imagine wanting to win that badly," Iola said.

"I can understand stealing prizes," Kathryn Soesbee said. "What I don't understand is Mr. Magnum. He was one of the contest's sponsors."

"That was the second tricky thing," Joe said. "We kept thinking that someone was causing this trouble trying to win prizes—when, in fact, Magnum was trying to keep people from winning prizes."

"Specifically, he was trying to keep anyone from winning the Geronimo motorcycle," Frank added.

"He must have promised it as a prize and then realized he couldn't really afford it," Callie said.

"That's what Con Riley, our friend down at the Police Department, thinks, after a preliminary check of Magnum's finances," Joe said.

"Backing out would have given his shop a lot of adverse publicity," Frank added. "And he was already struggling to make ends meet. Backing out could have put him out of business."

"So Harley Bettis and the Kings didn't have anything to do with any of this?" Iola said.

"Well, Missy and Jay may have put out the lights and released the bats at the party," Joe replied. "But that might have been Takei as well."

"We think that Magnum was using Bettis as a decoy—someone who could be blamed for any crimes that Magnum was committing," Frank said. "Magnum was pretty careful to make sure Bettis had no alibi when Magnum was doing his dirty work."

"That's rotten," Daphne said, "hiring someone just to make him a fall guy."

"With his record, Bettis was tailor-made for the part," Chet said.

"He's been trying to stay clean though," Frank said. "We even saw him try to shoo Missy Gates away from his workplace, though at the time, we thought the two of them were up to something shady. Ironic that he was trying so hard to hold on to a job working for a guy who was trying to frame him."

"So who broke into my vault and locked you all in?" asked Ms. Soesbee.

"That was Magnum," Joe said. "Nothing being stolen from the vault puzzled us. But he didn't need to take anything—he only needed to check on which clues led to the Geronimo cycle. That way, he could change them and throw people off."

"He changed the clue in the old dock warehouse so that no one could follow it," Callie said. "But we almost caught him at it—just like we almost caught him in your vault."

"With his experience in auto and cycle repair, hot-wiring Dracula's Dragster was a piece of cake," Joe said.

"Working with car and cycle keys also gave him the skills to pick the Book Bank's door lock once he lured Chet out to pick up the pizza that none of you ordered," Frank added.

"Clever guy," Callie said.

"Last night, he pretended to have been robbed of his own clues," Frank said, "when, in fact, he'd burned the clues himself in a barrel behind his shop just before we showed up. It was just another attempt to keep clues to the cycle out of players' hands."

"He used his own security system—which he'd conveniently left without recording tape—to spot us coming into the store, and go into his knocked-out act for us," Joe said. "Like Callie said: clever."

"But not clever enough to avoid the long arm of the law—in the form of Joe and Frank Hardy," Chet said, raising his cup of coffee in a toast.

They all laughed.

"The Bayport Merchants Association is very

grateful," Kathryn Soesbee said. "They've decided to give you three one of the unclaimed prizes from the contest. Would you prefer flying lessons, or boating lessons?"

"Hmm," Callie said. "I'm thinking flying lessons. We'll have to talk that over." She gave Frank a quick hug.

The elder Hardy leaned back in his chair. "What do you know," he said. "We may not have won the big prize, but we ended up with a pretty nice treat after all."

"Yeah," Joe agreed, "we got the treat—but the *trick* was on Rod Magnum!"